you won't remember this

you won't remember this

KATE BLACKWELL ❧ STORIES

Southern Methodist University Press / Dallas

Requests for permission to reproduce material
from this work should be sent to:
Rights and Permissions
Southern Methodist University Press
PO Box 750415
Dallas, Texas 75275-0415

Some of the stories in this collection previously appeared, in slightly different form, in the following publications: "What We Do for Love" (as "Weaving") in *The Greensboro Review*; "Duckie's Okay" in *New Letters*; "My First Wedding" in *Nebraska Review*; "Carpe Diem" in *Prairie Schooner*; "Queen of the May" (as "To Dance Again") in *The Literary Review*; "The Obi Tree" (as "Yodeling") in *Agni*; "George, Nadia, Blaise" in *The Crescent Review*; "You Won't Remember This" (as "Idyll") in *Sojourner*; "Pepper Hunt" in *So To Speak, Tameme: New Writing from North America*, and *Falling Backwards: Stories of Fathers and Daughters*; and "The Secret Life of Peonies" in *Carve* and *Enhanced Gravity, An Anthology of Fiction by Women Writers in Washington, D.C.*

Cover photograph : Jupiter Images / Botanica
Jacket and text design by Kellye Sanford

Library of Congress Cataloging-in-Publication Data

Blackwell, Kate, 1941–
    You won't remember this : stories / by Kate Blackwell. — 1st ed.
        p. cm.
    Contents: My first wedding — The secret life of peonies — What we do for love — The obi tree — Pepper hunt — Duckie's okay — You won't remember this — George, Nadia, Blaise — Heartbeatland — Queen of the May — Carpe diem — The minaret.
    ISBN-13: 978-0-87074-515-7 (alk. paper)
    ISBN-10: 0-87074-515-8 (alk. paper)
    1. Middle class—Southern States—Fiction. I. Title.

PS3602.L3258Y68 2007
808'.042—dc22   2006051261

For Leni, Diana, and Greg—
with me through all the stories

Acknowledgments

My special thanks go to Susan Land and Michele Orwin for their friendship, insightful reading, and unflagging encouragement. Thanks also to Ann McLaughlin, Leslie Pietryzk, Catherine Mayo, Wendi Kaufman, and Mary Kay Zuravleff, who read a number of the stories and challenged me to make them better. I am grateful to the lovely people at the MacDowell Colony and the Virginia Center for Creative Arts, where some of the stories took shape. I owe much to Kathryn Lang, my editor, for her faith, wisdom, and superb editorial attention, as well as to George Ann Ratchford and Keith Gregory, the other stalwarts at Southern Methodist University Press, where I felt welcome from the beginning. Finally, I thank my children, Leni, Diana, and Gregory Zumas, and my husband, Felix Jakob, for surrounding me with safety while I wrote.

The voyage of discovery is not in seeking new landscapes but in having new eyes.
MARCEL PROUST

Contents

My First Wedding

❧

"Augusta is reading Proust this summer," my mother said, the way she might have announced that someone we knew was going to the beach or having her house painted. It was a sweltering June afternoon. The two of us were sitting on her screened porch drinking Cokes and eating cherries. "She's been saving him for her forties," my mother added. I was twenty-four, about to be married, and I nodded and thought, So this is what one does in middle age.

I had not laid eyes on my cousin Augusta for several years, but I felt a secret bond with her based on the fact, often mentioned in the family, that she had written sonnets when she was young. I, too, had notions of being a writer, not of sonnets but of stories, by which I meant those oblique Joycean epiphanies revered by college English professors at the time. Since she had married and settled in Chappaqua, New York, and had three sons and a wispy little daughter, Augusta had written nothing, so far as anybody knew, but she read everything, sending an endless stream of books down to her aunts and cousins in North Carolina. As for her tackling *À la recherche du temps perdu,* I must have said something appreciative because I remember my mother replying, "Proust isn't everybody's cup of tea," and taking a sip of Coke.

I was used to these remarks of hers. Augusta and I both fell into the category of persons my mother occasionally referred to as "too smart for their own good," though I knew she admired Augusta, as we all did, for her vast reading, her intelligence, her looks. She was considered the beauty of the family, whose women were for the most part spare and brown. Augusta was dark-haired, her face strikingly full and white with large black eyes and deeply indented lips that reminded my grandmother of Lynn Fontanne. Her round arms and ample bosom, too ample by family standards when she was a girl, were seen as enhancements as she got older, and my mother and aunt began to refer to her as statuesque.

She was an only child, something my mother liked to pity her for. The household in which she grew up in the tiny tobacco town of Parsons, North Carolina, included her parents and her father's two spinster sisters, both of whom were deaf and may have been responsible for the declamatory voice Augusta acquired at an early age. Her father died when Augusta was nine and after that the household consisted entirely of women, all of whom, including the cook, doted on Augusta. Everyone thought she would be glad to get away from all the doting, but when she went off to the Baptist women's college in Raleigh she became desperately homesick. Her mother, Aunt Mary, kept her letters and for years afterward would read them aloud to guests: *Dear Mamsy, this is worse even than Nicholas Nickleby.*

Oh Mamsy, I never knew real life could be so awful. I would rather be a governess! Everybody always enjoyed these painful literate letters, especially Aunt Mary, who laughed uncontrollably when she read them, though her eyes grew moist.

On my mother's porch that day I considered making a snappy remark in defense of Augusta, myself, and Proust, but it was boiling hot and I was in a despairing mood, having spent the morning opening wedding gifts and writing down in a little book the names of the gift-givers, to whom I would later write thank-you notes. The thought of the note-writing ahead weighed on me and the presents weighed on me as well. What would I do with all those silver salvers and china egg cups and sets of ceramic coasters? The array of dust collectors piling up on my mother's dining-room table seemed a dismal portent of my future. Did most brides feel this way? Had my mother?

In the end, all I said was, "I wonder if Augusta still writes."

"Writes? I shouldn't think so," my mother said. "She has her hands full with those children. And Peter isn't easy. I don't know how she finds time to read as much as she does."

Not a good omen. I took a handful of cherries.

"What made you think of Augusta?" I asked my mother.

She gave me a long, hard, steady look. "I always think of Augusta when there's a wedding."

Then she excused herself to go do something in the house, leaving me with the heat and the cherries and my life lying like a brick in my lap.

I was twelve, precocious and plump, when Augusta was married on a hot June Saturday. By the time my parents and I arrived, the sultry lobby of the Parsons HoJo's was filled with relatives dragging suitcases containing wrinkled organdy and seersucker. We had not been there a minute when my Aunt Caro appeared, glared around the little lobby with its orange plastic chairs and fake philodendron, and said with a heavy sigh, "Isn't it just like Augusta to do this to us?"

The remark was such a good one that my mother repeated it endlessly for the next two days, which is almost certainly the reason Augusta's wedding acquired the reputation of being "difficult." It is true that the heat was intense but everyone else had married in more or less the same weather, and there was certainly nothing to complain of in the wedding itself or the lavish reception that followed, on which my mother speculated Aunt Mary spent everything Uncle Tru had left her. Yet for years afterward, whenever there was a family gathering that involved heat or travel or any untoward stress, one of us, my mother or my aunt or I, was likely to remark with a knowing look, "Oh, this is nothing. Remember Augusta's wedding?"

It was also memorable as our family's first marriage to a northerner. After graduating from college, Augusta had gone to New York, following a family tradition begun by Great Aunt Faye, who attended Columbia Teachers College, and continued by my mother and Aunt Caro, who shared a one-bedroom on the Upper East Side for a year or two before the war. Augusta had been living in the city for several years, working as a gofer for a publisher, when we heard that she was engaged. Aunt Mary gamely told everyone that the groom-to-be was a Yankee, but one we would all "fall in love with." In fact, my mother told me later, Aunt Mary was mortified at Peter Devane's stiff northern manners, and it nearly killed her to think that Augusta would spend the rest of her life so far from Parsons. Apparently, it had never occurred to her that Augusta would meet any but southern boys in New York City.

Everyone else greeted the news with expressions of relief. To our knowledge, Augusta had not had a beau since Jack Easter, if you could call such a boy a beau. He and Augusta had gone to high school together in Parsons. Aunt Mary didn't know the family; they lived somewhere between the edge of town and the tobacco fields, and she took a dim view of the friendship. But Augusta was lonely growing up in that country town and the boy seemed harmless enough. He was as crazy about books as Augusta was, Aunt Mary told my mother, though she didn't know where that would get him given where he came from. Still, Jack Easter was exceptionally bright and everyone was shocked when he hanged himself from a hook in his father's toolshed. He had just turned sixteen.

Augusta took it very hard. She began writing sonnets about "ambrosial youth" and "perfect waste," sad, rhyming verses reflecting despair and Edna St. Vincent Millay. Aunt Mary didn't know what to do with the poems; she disapproved of their black tone as neither Christian nor sensible, but thought they were probably brilliant. Finally, she had them copied and sent to Great Aunt Faye, who taught Shakespeare in a county consolidated high school. Word of the sonnets spread. For a while, the family conceived of Augusta as a real poetess and spoke of her with new respect. I was surprised to find her, at family reunions, the same boisterous girl who liked to appear with a nylon stocking over her face to scare the children.

On that hot June Saturday in Parsons, I wasn't much concerned with the family view of Augusta's marriage. This was my
first out-of-town wedding and I was terribly excited. There was
the strangeness of staying in a motel: the carpeted corridors
reeking of disinfectant, the ice machine crunching out frozen
cubes at the end of our hall, the paper strip declaring our toilet
seat fit to be sat on. I was also pleased with my new dress for
the occasion, an apple green organdy, which had come with a
matching hair ribbon that had been left at home by mistake,
causing a brief, violent rupture between my mother and me.
Most of my thoughts, however, as we prepared for the great
event, were given over to expectations I had about a boy who
Aunt Mary had said, untruthfully as it turned out, was dying
to meet me. He was one of Augusta's cousins on the Truitt side,
and I had formed extravagant hopes based on Aunt Mary's
well-meant lie. The disappointment I was to suffer was entirely
my own fault. I had not yet understood the family view of romantic love as a grand fiction to be talked of constantly without the slightest concession to reality.

Until then, however, the wedding fulfilled my best hopes.
The Parsons Baptist Church was transformed with baby's
breath and white sweetheart roses. An organist had been im-
ported from Raleigh to impress the northern in-laws with
flawlessly rendered Handel and Grieg. While we waited for the
bride to appear, I thought about the boy I was to meet, who
must also be sitting somewhere in the church, possibly scout-
ing out girls, guessing which one was me. I felt a tingling in my
chest as I imagined his thin face and smoldering eyes, features

that belonged, I was to realize later, to my picture of the boy who killed himself.

I had spent considerable time, after Augusta's engagement was announced, thinking about Jack Easter. I envisioned him with the bony frame and sallow skin of the poor, a boy who read Twain and Steinbeck and Poe (books I too read from my parents' shelves) and was derided for it by the other students in his country school. I pictured him and Augusta, the brilliant outcast boy and the large lonely girl, walking together along the streets of the little town, past the drugstore and the hardware store and the bank where Uncle Tru had formerly presided, out to the tobacco fields. Here they found some private sandy lane where, according to my chaste scenario, they sat and talked about books.

Later, Augusta would return to the house on Main Street, to the doting mother and oblivious aunts, while Jack Easter walked home through the fields, deaf to the pleas of doves and wind soughing in the distant pines, sounds he once had loved. He understood that they could not marry, given the great social gulf between them, and his brilliant, uncanny mind foretold everything I was now witnessing—the magnificent wedding, the church drenched in the scent of gardenias, the stranger waiting at the altar—and he went home and hanged himself.

Then the first chords of Mendelssohn's March boomed out and Augusta, pale and statuesque in ivory satin, paced with great dignity down the center aisle on Uncle Alec's arm, recapturing for that moment in my eyes her old aura as tragic poetess. All at once, I felt that I *pined,* though for what or whom I didn't know. What does one know at the age of twelve? I still wore patent leather flats and would not start to menstruate for another year, though my breasts were tender and I had desperate dreams of love.

After the ceremony was over, we all got in our cars and drove three blocks to the Women's Club, a one-story yellow stucco with miniature pillars and portico. On a sweltering flagstone terrace, a band of middle-aged white men tooted out swing and the younger people congregated: my cousin Scottie, a bevy of teenaged Truitts, none of whom remotely resembled the boy I expected, and I. My mother and father were seated on the terrace at a long table with Aunt Caro and Uncle Webb, Uncle Alec, and Great Aunt Kat's daughters, who were more or less Augusta's age, all having what looked to be a riotous good time. I remember my mother laughing hysterically as my father called out in a fake roguish voice his demands that the band play "Beautiful Brown Eyes."

Augusta and Peter Devane joined them when the receiving line was finished. Augusta had abandoned her dignified manner and was acting the outrageous clown. She sat on Uncle Alec's lap and bounced up and down to general hilarity and Alec's great discomfort—he claimed later she had burst something permanently, though he left it to us to imagine whether it was his spleen or his cummerbund. To my aunt across the table, she bellowed, "Lord, Caro! Don't you wish F. Scott were here?" Leaning forward with her large white face and glittering black eyes, she pronounced, "You know what? If my life were a nineteenth-century novel, it would be over." Then she laughed uproariously. Someone might have thought she was drunk if Aunt Mary had allowed anything other than fruit punch and iced mint tea to be served. Finally, my father got up and asked Augusta to dance, leaving my mother to entertain Peter Devane. "He told me all about *chemicals*," she reported later, as though only a Yankee would know no better than to talk about something of substance at his own wedding.

Still, everybody was determined to like Peter Devane. He was tall and blond, "patrician" was Aunt Caro's word for him, though a little stiff, which was understandable since he was meeting Augusta's relatives en masse for the first time. And it was universally agreed that he adored Augusta. He watched her with a half smile on his lips as though in a state of perpetual amazement. He had gone to Groton and Harvard, and his politics were assumed to be terrible—it was years before we found out he had been a Democrat all the time. But at the wedding, nobody wanted to find out too much about Peter Devane for fear of what it would be. Everyone was relieved when my grandmother remarked with finality, "Their children will be stunning."

As for the elder Devanes, the generally held view was that *he* had a sense of humor, or would have had one if *she* had let him. This opinion was never verified since the in-laws returned to upstate New York immediately after the wedding and never came south again. I remember them as a tall, austere couple seated for the reception at an indoor table with Augusta's deaf aunts and Great Aunt Faye. Apparently, Faye wore herself out entertaining the Devanes and had to take the summer off from teaching. My mother always referred to her conduct at Augusta's wedding as heroic.

What I myself endured at the reception can only be de-scribed as a painful skirmish with real life. Though the boy did appear and dance with me, having been primed by his Truitt aunts, he turned out to be short, red-faced, and clumsy. He managed in the course of ten minutes to crush my small right toe and spill punch down the front of my new dress. "Sorry," he muttered, lifting his upper lip to expose a shield of metal brac-es. He must have been in agony, too, but that realization did not come to me until much later and would not have helped at the time. In the midst of the sultry blooming night of Augusta's wedding, my waist and hand clasped by the boy's hot palms as we moved heavily to imitation Duke Ellington, I yearned more than I had ever yearned for anything in my life to be reading a good book.

My suffering went unnoticed, however. What everyone chiefly remembered about Augusta's wedding was that the bride and groom refused to leave. Since nobody else could go until they did, the party went on and on while the band played slower and slower like a music box winding down until Aunt Mary almost collapsed from the effort of keeping it all going. Her pink face acquired the ruddy glow of desperation as she marched from table to table, demanding, "Is everybody getting enough to eat?" Finally Aunt Faye got up and went to speak to Augusta, who even then made no move until my mother and Caro rose, took Augusta by the arms, and the three of them disappeared into the warren of club offices where a dressing room had been set up.

And then time stopped. At least, the door to the dressing room remained closed for what seemed an eternity to those outside, where the reception staggered on in the insufferable heat, the exhausted band playing to the two or three couples who still swayed wearily on the terrace, Aunt Faye dredging up yet another family anecdote with which to entertain the now speechless in-laws, Aunt Mary moving like a sleepwalker from table to table where guests drooped like wilted roses over their punch cups, while Peter Devane in his white suit furiously paced the foyer.

For me, the waiting had the endless, inevitable quality of nightmare. The young people with whom I had been sitting had long since drifted away, all but the chunky boy, my thirteen-year-old "date," who unaccountably remained in his chair beside me, staring with glazed eyes at his empty cup. We had not spoken for ages, not since I had asked inanely what teams he played on at his school and he had replied miserably that he was in the band. Finally, I found the courage to rise. For a moment I stood there in my soiled dress, my hair limp and cheeks burning. I wanted to say something that would make it all right, to end the sorry spectacle we made with a graceful gesture of farewell. "I've got to go" was what came out. The boy continued to stare downward, another victim of family myths I suppose. I walked away.

I meant to beg my father to take me back to the motel, but when I found him, before I could open my mouth, he hissed, "Where the deuce is your mother?" in a voice I had never heard him use before. Without replying, I ran away to the back of the clubhouse, where I hid in one of the empty rooms, filled with self-loathing and despair.

Lying on a dusty couch, I became aware of voices. Then a

braying laugh let me know that I was next door to the bride's dressing room. I got up and tested the door between the two rooms. It was unlocked. I cracked it softly, feeling a thrill as I did so.

"*Lord*," I heard Augusta cry, "did you see Uncle Walter and Aunt Kat double dipping on the dance floor. I thought I'd *die*."

My mother told me later that from the moment they entered that hot, stuffy little room Augusta would not, or could not, stop talking and pacing in her tight-fitting gown, clasping and unclasping her shapely hands.

"I *told* Mother the Truitts would try to take over this wedding. They're here in absolute masses."

My mother and Aunt Caro tried to persuade Augusta to undress and put on her pink linen going-away suit. "Everybody's waiting for you and Peter to leave," Caro said pointedly. "You have to get changed."

My mother rummaged in the overnight bag for the appropriate lingerie. "What on earth are these?" she demanded, pulling several sheets of paper from among pairs of silk stockings. On the pages were neatly typed the titles and authors of hundreds of books.

"My reading for the next fifty years," Augusta replied and dropped her wedding gown like a rag onto the floor.

My mother and Caro began scanning the papers and only looked up when they realized that Augusta had collapsed onto a chair, shaking with sobs. After a moment, my mother went over and laid a hand on her heaving shoulder and asked, "Augusta, is it Peter?"

Caro threw her a warning look, but my mother plunged

ahead. "You don't have to go away with him, you know. It's not too late even now."

"What on earth are you talking about, Anna?" Caro hissed.

My mother turned fiercely to her. "Don't you remember when you said the same thing to me? It was two days before my wedding. I've never forgotten it."

"Of course I remember. When I walked in and saw you lying there with your face all red and puffy, naturally I thought— Nobody told me you'd just had your wisdom teeth out."

"But what if it *had* been what you thought?" My mother's voice rose. "What if I *hadn't* wanted to go through with it? You offered me a way out. I can hear you now: *Anna, you don't have to marry that man!*"

At that moment Augusta moaned loudly, and my mother, as she explained later, concluded that she had spoken hastily. Augusta was simply overwrought. In the next moment, it occurred to her that Augusta had moaned a name.

Behind my door, I puzzled at the silence that fell then between my mother and aunt, broken only by Augusta's sobs and her muttered repetition of what sounded to me like *shan't, shan't, shan't.* I thought she was refusing to go away with Peter Devane, using the Dickensian language she was famous for. My mother and Caro heard her repeating a name: *Jack.*

It did not surprise my mother or my aunt that Augusta was thinking of the boy who died. That was what romantic love was all about. They too had had their flings with all that, but they were older now and knew those feelings could not be indulged. Peter Devane was a perfectly harmless man and Jack Easter was dead.

"We have to get her dressed," my mother told Caro.

They both looked at Augusta, who was still crying.

"I'll be right back," my aunt whispered and slipped out of the room.

She returned a few minutes later with a small silver flask of whisky. My mother stared. The only people at the wedding who were not teetotaling Baptists were teetotaling Presbyterians. Perhaps the groom's friends had smuggled in liquor, but it was inconceivable that Caro had approached one of them. To add to the mystery, Caro said vehemently before my mother could speak, "Never ask me where I got this." It wasn't until years later, after his early death, that we learned Uncle Webb was an alcoholic and, even then, it was a friend who let us know. Caro never uttered a word.

However, at the Parsons Women's Club that heavy, humid June night, my uncle's sad fate still lay in the future and his whisky saved the day. My mother and Caro administered a thimble's worth to Augusta, who gagged, choked, and had to stop crying in order to breathe. While she struggled for air, the other two sat down and waited. After a while, Augusta blotted her tears and lifted her large, red-stained face, reminding my mother less of a bride or tragic poetess than of Raggedy Ann. She and my aunt burst out laughing. After a moment, Augusta laughed, too. Then the three of them began a lively conversation about books.

At this point, I pushed the door open another inch or two so that I could peer into the room. The tableau I saw was worthy of a painting by a Dutch master. The background was obscured in shadow so that the eye was drawn ineluctably to the three figures sitting in a circle of light. Augusta wore nothing but her ivory slip; her bare arms and throat gleamed like porcelain in the glare of the single bulb. My mother in scarlet silk leaned toward her across the table, her lips parted in mid-speech. Beside her, my aunt smiled mysteriously, her brown hair braided and wound around her head in a burnished coronet. Between them on the table were spread the titles of books that were to sustain Augusta through her married life. My heart beat with longing. These women were the most beautiful sight I had ever seen.

"*All* of Fielding!" my aunt exclaimed. "Isn't that overdoing it?"

"Who on earth is Huysmans?" asked my mother.

"Is O. Douglas here? You *must* have O. Douglas!"

"I thought you hated Mary Roberts Rinehart."

"*All* of Conan Doyle!"

The litany went on, as the flask also made the rounds, its cap fastened to a short chain that tinkled musically each time it was removed.

"Dreiser's depressing but worth it."

Tinkle, tinkle.

"The Katherine Mansfield stories are so sad."

"You'll love Storm Jameson's latest."

"*All* of Zola!"

Tinkle, tinkle.

"Can you believe I've never read Sarah Orne Jewett?"

"Well, shame on you."

They all laughed. The chain tinkled.

"What about Anne Morrow Lindbergh?" Augusta demanded. "Is she good or sappy?"

My mother cried, "Good!" as Caro declaimed, "Sappy!" They collapsed in laughter.

Tinkle, tinkle.

It was then that my mother saw me at the door and let out a shriek. "What is *that*?" She pointed at the large stain on my dress, the gift of my prince. "Oh, hush, Anna," my aunt said and beckoned me in. So I, too, entered the room and became part of the tableau, a disheveled young girl in a green dress, grinning broadly, proud to be part of the picture, without the slightest idea of what was really going on.

The revel ended when Great Aunt Faye flung open the door. She reported to the family, later, that we were laughing our fool heads off.

A dozen years later, on another hot June Saturday, I attended another wedding, in an elegant little white and gold chapel. The groom was a dark-haired, pleasant-looking man in his late twenties. The bride beaming under a cascade of Brussels lace was myself. How I got there I had no clear notion, but I knew as I entered the little butter-colored chapel, Lilith-like on my father's arm, that no passion had brought me; I was playing my part in a gorgeous fiction. The marriage ended some years later, the first divorce in our family, which greatly shamed my mother. I would catch her on occasion staring at me with narrowed eyes as though at a stranger who had appeared mysteriously in our midst.

My mother and I never discussed my divorce, beyond the dry facts I gave her at the time. Her single question was: "What do I tell people?" On the surface, our relations continued as they had always been. We sat on her porch drinking Cokes and eating cherries while she caught me up on family news: Augusta's latest novel recommendation; Aunt Caro's move to a house in the country, against the advice of nearly everyone; Aunt Mary's decision to go into a retirement home instead of moving north to live with Augusta and Peter. All these events are long in the past now. It has been forty years since Augusta's wedding.

The last time I saw her was at a family event when she was in her early fifties, as I am now. She wore a loose flowered muu-muu and flip-flops on her feet revealing crimson-polished nails. Her black hair showed a streak of pure white. As she and I chatted, the book lists came into my mind and I almost asked her whether she had finished them. This was before my divorce, when I myself had two young children, had written nothing in years, and was laid waste by misery at the way my life had turned out. I had a great urge to ask Augusta about her marriage to Peter Devane, whether she had been happy with him, and about the lost boy Jack Easter, whether she still thought of him, whether she loved him. I wanted to remind her of her wedding and that stuffy little room, to recall her tears, the laughter, the tinkling of the flask. It all seemed suddenly so important. But of course I didn't. Time had swept us so far beyond those moments, I had no idea whether she even remembered them or what significance they had for her if she did.

Then she asked, "Are you doing any writing?"

I stared at her, the blood rushing to my face.

"I always thought you'd write," she went on, in a strange, forced voice. "You seemed so determined. Mama and Faye were sure you'd do something along those lines. They used to talk about you all the time. I was madly jealous."

I could hardly believe what I was hearing. Was this what the family thought of me?

"To tell the truth, I was surprised when you got married." Augusta's eyes avoided mine as she said this, and her face tightened as though with pain. Then her lips, those deeply indented lips my grandmother had admired, spread into a smile. "*Lord,* listen to me. You have those darling little girls and that handsome husband." And she laughed the loud musical laugh I remembered from my childhood, only now it seemed riven with something terrible, grief or desperation. Or perhaps it was my own confusion I was hearing. At any rate, I couldn't speak and apparently she did not expect me to. She glanced away toward the other side of the room where Peter Devane, tall and whitehaired, was telling some story to my mother and aunt, who were listening with cautious smiles. Without another word, she walked off.

Today I sat on my mother's porch as we talked of Augusta's death, at sixty-eight, of cancer. I had not seen her again after our strange encounter, though I often thought of her, as when I spent a winter curled up with Proust. I regret that my own daughters never knew her and would not now easily understand if I tried to tell them about her. They would find her life banal, I am sure, and as distant from their own as those intimate interiors by Hals or Vermeer. I, however, have learned to appreciate the beauty of still lives, and it saddens me to think they will be lost. For who will remember women like my mother, my aunt, and Augusta? Who will remember any of us who live so hidden, so far from nearly everything?

The Secret Life of Peonies

ℰ

Alexandra arranges six pink shrimp on a white plate, adds a sprig of cilantro, a handful of lemony arugula, a single cherry tomato. Tommy smiles up at her as she sets the plate in front of him. His face is pink, like the shrimp, his hair a coppery red. Then: *clank,* Saturday's mail shoots through the mail slot in the hall. Tommy shoves back his chair with a shriek of wood on tile.

"Where are you going? We're having lunch," Alexandra says.

"Just getting the mail, sweetheart."

Alexandra tenses. She grew up in a home where you did not leave the table until the meal was over, no matter what happened. The ceiling could collapse and Alexandra and her parents would still sit in their reproduction Queen Anne chairs eating fricasseed chicken and plaster. Nor did you read your mail during a meal. Tommy, despite that Princeton degree, was not brought up with these rules.

She arranges her own plate and carries it to the table, sits down, takes a sip of cool white wine. The kitchen in this mid-

day light could be a photograph in a magazine. Sunlight warms
the Mexican tiles, brings out their rich caramel tones, while
silvering the pale wood grain of the table, the granite counter-
tops. She sees herself in the photograph, a slim woman in white
capri pants, face half hidden because she is looking down. She
looks up. She would never allow her house to be photographed
for a magazine. They are private people. Still. She looks down
at the white plate, the shrimp in their forest of green, that single sphere of red.

Tommy returns, his face now a mottled crimson. He is
holding a sheet of paper. A tiny quiver, like sex, slithers through
Alexandra's abdomen. Something has happened. The investment company, she knows, is downsizing; even managers are
getting pink slips, though it's unthinkable that Tommy would
get one. He is responsible for huge portfolios; his clients adore
him. Anyway, those things don't come in the mail, do they?
Maybe it's another wheedling letter from his sister trying to get
them to spend a week this summer in her un-air-conditioned
house in the Poconos. Something tells Alexandra the letter is
not from his sister. Or the company.

She reaches out and takes it, white copy paper, the shiny
kind she doubts a financial institution would stock. Ordinary
people buy it in bulk at Staples. She reads the single sentence
slowly as though she is parsing a foreign language: *You—
may—be—interested—to know—your wife—is having—an
affair—with. . . .* A cloud drifts over the man's name. She blinks.
Her vision clears. Tommy is looking at her, hunching his shoulders as though he's waiting for a ball to slice toward him over
the net, waiting to slice it back.

"Who could have written this garbage?" she says. And sees him straighten. He has recognized her voice: cool, deliberate, very effective with potential donors at the museum. She crumples the paper and throws it on the floor. "What twisted mind—", then watches as he bends and picks up the letter.

"Tommy, you cannot believe this craziness."

Her voice is less cool now, though not panicked, more the concerned tone a mother might use to calm a child. You aren't afraid of the dark, darling. There's nothing to be afraid of. Why, nothing's *there.*

"No," he says and smoothes the paper between his hands. "But we shouldn't ruin the evidence."

"Evidence of what? We should burn this!"

"The guy exists, I presume."

"Mead Latourette?" She forces herself to say the name that has been typed at the end of the sentence. "He owns a gallery. He's on one of our committees. I *know* him—"

She looks down. The light has shifted, leaving the expensive tiles darkly muddy. After all, they *are* mud. She gets up and walks out of the room.

She sits on the terrace holding a cup of coffee. Tommy has gone off to his tennis game—they agreed he should go; the letter is an obscene joke by some loony; they will forget it: this decided after she returned to the kitchen in tears, after he held and soothed her, after they finished the by then slightly too warm lunch wine. Nausea stirs Alexandra's stomach, where the wine now lies. She clenches her teeth and stares at her roses—pink Queen Elizabeths, red Princess Graces, a peach-

tone Cary Grant—and the mixed beds of white and gold dai-
sies, blue cornflowers, lilies in all hues. Women in her family
have always been avid gardeners. Alexandra spends hours on
weekends taking care of her flowers, while Tommy is busy with
tennis, squash, handball, you name it.

Clustered next to the terrace are her favorites, the peonies—
she could touch one droopy leaf with her foot if she wanted
to—their buds swollen fat, waiting for the warm May sun to
burst them open. Right now, each bud is swarming with ants,
which play some mysterious role in the life of peonies. She read
somewhere that the flowers produce a sugary juice ants like,
but what do the peonies get in return? Do those busy black
insects enhance the peonies' beauty? Or are they just selfish
sybarites? Alexandra believes they help. One year, she carefully
dusted all the ants off and the buds stayed closed tight as fists
and never bloomed.

She puts the peonies out of her mind and tries to focus on
the vicious letter, but her mind is closed tight, like the buds,
while in those teeming regions of her inner self, she feels panic,
fear, a touch of hysteria. Stay calm, she tells herself. It will be all
right. She sets her cup down, cold coffee sloshing into the saucer, anger replacing fear. (She thinks she knows who wrote the
letter—the little slut!) But they will get through this. There will
be a period of tension, a few bad days. Naturally, Tommy feels
outraged. He believes the letter writer is someone he knows—
the writer used his full name on the envelope: Thomas E.
Parrish. She forbore from pointing out that this name is in the
phone book.

She remembers Tommy's long white legs in his white tennis shorts as he paced over the Mexican tiles, his porcelain skin sprinkled with pale orange freckles and fine red hairs, so unlike Mead Latourette's smooth beige skin and sturdy limbs. She shivers in the sun. She needs to lie down in her darkened bedroom with a damp cloth on her forehead. She stares at the peony bud near her foot, its skin of moving ants. The lunch wine begins to rise. She leaps up and rushes into the house.

Mead Latourette is an inch or two shorter than Alexandra. His dark hair falls to his collar, his fringe of beard gives his round face a slightly sinister look, ironically, since Mead is the most genial of men. He comes from Alabama, of Cajun descent, and speaks with a laconic cadence which, the first time she heard it, on the terrace of the Washington Hilton, made her whoop with laughter. *You look like somebody I def'nitely ought to know.* She likes to repeat the remark, to tease him. He likes to repeat her whoop. Alexandra, at thirty-eight, tall and coltish, with long auburn hair and a small delicate face (a Filippo Lippi Virgin's, Mead says), doesn't look like a woman who makes loud sounds. And she doesn't, often. On the hotel terrace—prelunch drinks at a seminar on art bequests—he circled back with two glasses of wine. "For the cool lady with the hot laugh," he said, handing her one. "What say we play hooky?" The invitation, she is still convinced, surprised him, too.

Now Mead says in an appalled whisper on the phone, "Run that by me again, cherie."

Alexandra does, in a flat voice as though she were reading his horoscope: *You may be interested to know*—

"Who the devil—?"

"I thought you might—"

"If I knew I'd kill him."

"Or her," Alexandra says. (Surely he can guess the culprit.)

"Or her," he amends. "How is Tom taking this?"

"I told him it was garbage. He's all right."

Though Tommy is not all right. He lost badly at tennis on Saturday and got sloppy drunk at dinner that night—dinner she did not eat because of the stomachache that came with the lunch wine. On Sunday they hardly spoke. Today is Monday, the first chance she has had to call Mead, safely, from her office at the museum (door tightly shut) to his at his gallery, the Obelisk.

"I take it that you—that Franny—didn't get a letter."

Franny is Mead's wife, a compact blonde with muscular legs. Alexandra has seen her at receptions at the Obelisk. They've even chatted. Franny is an amateur cellist, a health fanatic, also a devoted mother to their two daughters, aged fourteen and eleven. Mead refers to all three as "my girls." "I live a desperately domestic life, cherie," he likes to assure Alexandra. When he's not hobnobbing with artists, she likes to tease, wheeling and dealing in Georgetown and Adams Morgan, coddling and cajoling over Moët and Coors. To her teasing, Mead spreads his hands, those smooth ash-colored fingers, as his eyebrows peak like tents. "Gotta make a living, baby lamb."

The surprising fact, to her, is that she and Mead spend so much of their time together talking about their other lives, their spouses, their houses, their weekends. He describes his daughters' soccer games, family bowling trips, his clipping of a very unruly hedge. At the neighborhood barbecues Franny likes to throw, Mead presides over a gas grill. In an apron? Yes, of course, in an apron. "My Cajun chicken is to die for," he brags. "You should try Tommy's swordfish with herbs," Alexandra can't resist replying.

She tells Mead about Tommy's tennis matches—she fell in love watching him play for Princeton, those long legs, that determined jaw, the quick grin in her direction when he won a set. There was a time when she envisioned a life on the circuit, herself in the stands wearing a fabulous hat and sunglasses. Investment banking, however, has its compensations, her new kitchen tiles for one. Also, the sailing they used to do until she made Tommy sell the boat. She couldn't stand the tiny bunks, the constant demands for care that were worse than a child's. "But now you feel guilty," Mead suggests wisely. "Yes," she confesses.

There is also the matter of the real children she and Tommy have decided not to have. "And why do you think you don't want them?" Mead is concerned. He wouldn't want to be the cause for such a decision. But he has nothing to do with it. It's because she has too many selfish desires: her garden, her house, her job. Her own mother used to tell her she was selfish—*You think of nobody but yourself, Alexandra*—when she came in after curfew, making her father ill from worry; when she refused to continue piano lessons, breaking her mother's heart. Well, all right, she is selfish. She doesn't *want* children. Tommy did at first but now he agrees with her. They are happy as things are. "Then why do you look so sad, cherie?" She begins to cry. Of course, she can never be *sure*. Mead holds her while she sobs. These are the moments she cherishes, not just the sex. If it were just the sex, it would have been over by now. Surely.

They agree that Tommy and Franny will never be hurt by the single hour of pleasure and companionship they enjoy every week—sometimes, actually, more than an hour (lately, closer to two, even three hours, once an entire incredible afternoon)—because they will never know. No one will.

Though it appears someone does.

Mead takes a deep breath. "No letter at our house."

"We need to talk."

"Ahhhhh, sweetheart. We're leaving tomorrow for the Gulf."

"I remember," she says coldly. Mead and his girls are going on vacation, somewhere south, near water. They will be away a week.

The pause lengthens. Finally, Mead says in a different voice, "You're right, cherie. Noon at the deli?"

The Lebanese deli off Dupont Circle is where they went that first time they played hooky and stayed for hours, leaning toward each other over little dishes of garlicky hummus and cucumbers and glasses of minty tea, exchanging opinions so thrillingly in sync about Rauschenberg's mixed messages, Frankenthaler's genius, Schnabel's triviality. Afterward, they walked along tree-shaded streets lined with townhouses set in immaculate gardens of impatiens and box, one of which housed the Obelisk, where Mead's assistant, Paige, was holding the fort. He referred to her as "the child," though Alexandra, who has seen Paige many times since, suspects "the child" is closing in on thirty. She has had her suspicions about Paige ever since that first day, when Mead took such pains to avoid walking past the gallery. On another street, he drew Alexandra into the shadow of a holly tree and kissed her so deeply she had to pull away, finally, to breathe.

They still meet at the deli occasionally, in memory of that first time, two years ago. *Two years,* Alexandra marvels.

"Not at the deli," she says now. "At Didier's."

"Ahhhhh, sweetheart—"

Quickly, before he can say more, she hangs up.

All Alexandra knows about Mead's friend Didier is that he is never home for lunch. His apartment is furnished like a hotel suite with white furniture, beige carpets. On the tables are French periodicals, on the walls pale prints of orchids. The single blast of color comes from the plum-colored sheets on the king-sized bed. In this bed, among these purple sheets, they have just made swift sweaty love and now lie entwined, Mead's thick brown legs stretched across Alexandra's slim white ones. She is turned on her side, one arm slung over his chest, her head on his pillowy shoulder. She loves Mead naked. Clothed, he has a professorial air, but in bed he turns boyish. Often he vaults onto the mattress, bouncing with high glee.

The first time she saw him do this, she blurted, "You really like this, don't you?"

"Oh I *do.* I like *you* so much."

Before Mead, Alexandra viewed sex as a matter of high seriousness—akin to going to church, she has realized, with some amusement. The only child of strict Presbyterians, her father a doctor, her mother a housewife whose career was raising a perfect daughter, Alexandra is surprised she isn't frigid. She probably would be if she had not discovered, when she was sixteen, squeezed into the backseat of a smelly Ford with a sweet boy who adored her, that sex was where a perfect daughter could be like anybody else without anyone seeing her—except the boy, of course.

But lovemaking with Mead is so nonserious, so richly antic, so profoundly enjoyable, she feels—has felt from the beginning—there can be nothing dangerous here, nothing hurtful, nothing *wrong*. It's not an affair they are having—Alexandra dislikes the word: it sounds cheap, self-indulgent, *tabloid;* they are having something else, something she admittedly has no word for but would, if asked, describe as healthy, human, even, obscurely, *right*. Now she sniffs the familiar nutty aroma of his skin and traces with her finger the fierce curve of a rib. What would she do without him? This hateful letter cannot mean they will have to stop seeing each other.

"You've been through hell, haven't you?" he says.

"You mean I look like hell?" She withdraws her hand.

"You look beautiful. You *are* beautiful." He is gazing at her sideways, his lips puckered thoughtfully. "Who do you think is onto us?"

"Nobody," she says. "They can't be."

"Haven't you told anyone? A friend?"

"Who would I tell? All my friends are jealous of me as it is."

Mead's eyebrows rise, but it's true; the women she knows are always remarking on her lovely house, her sweet husband, her interesting job. Only the tragedy of no children, as she knows her friends think of it, redeems her in their eyes.

"Really," she says. "I haven't told anyone."

"How about the museum? Anybody mention your long lunches?"

"My director assumes I'm out wooing big bucks. My secretary's grateful for the extra time on the phone with her boyfriend."

She pauses in exasperation. Does he really *not* know who wrote the letter?

"What about one of your old loves?" she says. "What about that artist woman Franny found out about?"

"That was ten years ago. I don't even know where she lives now. Besides, she wouldn't."

"Well, is there any—?"

"As I have told you many times, cherie, whether you believe it or not, I am a monogamist."

"Monogamy" is an odd choice of words, but Alexandra knows what he means. She is not jealous of Franny, but if Mead were making love to another woman not his wife, *that* would be unbearable.

She suspects Mead had a fairly active sex life before he married Franny—someone of his huge attractiveness, his great appreciation of sex, must have had. He has admitted to only one liaison after marriage, an artist, older than he (so is Alexandra, by a year), a talented woman, not terribly successful professionally, but very sensually alive, very—if Alexandra were jealous of anyone, it would be this woman. But it ended disastrously. Franny found out through a careless phone call and, well, cherie, the sky fell in. Franny's milk dried up—their second daughter was nursing—and their older daughter, then four, woke crying in the night for months. Franny cried. The baby cried. Mead cried. It was a terrible time that showed him how important his family was to him, how he can't bear to hurt them again, which Alexandra understands. She would not want to hurt Tommy either. Still. She thinks of ants and peonies and a barely perceptible shiver glides over her skin. There is a lesson there if she only knew what it was.

"Could Franny have found out?" she asks now.

"Trust me," Mead says. "I would def'nitely know."

He shifts to his side. Alexandra stretches out on her back. He lifts a strand of her hair and examines it, twisting it carefully around his finger.

"Maybe we should take a small break," he says.

Her breathing slows, fog envelops her brain.

"A break?" she whispers.

"To be on the safe side."

The safe side? What side is that? The side of her next to him feels hot as though he is an electric heater, the kind you buy for those awful little uninsulated houses, the kind that blows up and incinerates you. *Safe?*

"We'll be back a week from Thursday," he says. "I'll call. We'll talk."

She refuses to look at him or to speak.

"Alexandra," he says. "Ahhhh, sweetheart—" Then he rolls away from her over the purple sheets, taking all the heat with him.

That night, Alexandra and Tommy sit at their kitchen table with the letter between them, making a list of possible letter writers. They examine the paper, its size and shape, its flimsiness. It was written on a PC, printed on a DeskJet, not very professionally. Courier font—who uses Courier these days? A woman must have written it, Tommy declares. Alexandra says nothing. She is feeling ill again. Her digestion has not returned to normal since the letter. On the other hand, Tommy says, the language is more like a man's, brief, to the point. She shrugs. Her throat fills. She rushes off to the bathroom. How degrading, she thinks, as she kneels by the toilet. Can this crouching, spewing woman be *she?* She curls up on the floor and closes her eyes.

The next day, she walks past the Obelisk, turns, walks past again. The door is open and Paige flits by, twitching her hips, holding a cigarette in one hand. The "child" is not beautiful, too thin, too pop-eyed, but adoration can be a kind of aphrodisiac and, clearly, Paige adores Mead. Alexandra has watched her at openings, in her dead-black blouse and stamp-sized skirt, circling him like a moth. Paige has the second sight of the besotted. Otherwise, how to account for her childish behavior toward Alexandra, the phone messages for Mead not delivered, the scalding stares when Alexandra and Mead exchange private words at a reception, the wine spilled on Alexandra's shoes a few weeks ago as Paige rushed by. *Oh Mrs. Parrish, I'm so-o-o sorry.* Of course she wrote the letter.

Paige appears again and flicks the cigarette out into the yard. Is it the cigarette that does it? The careless littering? Driven by a rage she never knew she possessed, Alexandra crosses the street and enters the gallery. Paige has arranged herself on a chair in front of a huge painting of a male nude in lumpy red pastiche and is pretending to study a catalogue. Alexandra stations herself before a blue version of the same male.

Finally, there is the squeak of a chair and a shrill "Oh, Mrs. Parrish! Is there something—?"

Alexandra whirls. "Yes?"

"He's not here. He's out of town." Paige sounds terrified. "He's—May I help you?"

Guilt stains her foolish face. Alexandra wants to strike her, to immolate her. She says briskly, "I must have mistaken the day. Tell me, do you have a computer here?"

"No. I mean, it's not working."

"Ah." She stares coolly at Paige. "But you *do* do letters."

Paige's mouth opens, but Alexandra is already walking out. As she crosses the street, she looks back in time to see "the child" close the gallery door. Does she slam it shut with her little rump? Alexandra thinks she does.

That night, again, she and Tommy sit in their kitchen and go over the letter, its texture and tone, the extra spaces between words seen as somehow significant. Tommy is again convinced the perpetrator is a woman. A jealous woman friend of Alexandra's. Or no, more likely a gal at the investment company, someone he's pissed off without realizing it. He mentions a Julie in REITs, a Sharon in corporate bonds, neither of whom could possibly know Mead Latourette. But Tommy appears to have forgotten Mead entirely.

So it's a shock when he says, as he spears a tomato, "Babe, tell me about this Latourette. What's he like?"

The piece of steak she's chewing turns to leather. "Mead?"

Tommy nods encouragingly. "What's the fellow like? You said you know him."

"Oh." She tries to think what Mead is like. "His gallery's so-so successful. He does American Expressionism. It's not all that *in* right now."

"Married?"

"I think so. Yes. I met his wife at a gallery opening once. That was, gosh, two years ago."

Tommy looks at her. She feels her face redden. Her father used to look at her like that. *Alexandra, are you telling me the truth? You did not leave the dance before it ended? You came straight home?* It strikes her that this is not the first time Tommy has reminded her of her father. They finish the meal in silence.

She is sitting at her desk when Mead calls. "All tanned and fat from beignets?" she says in her cool museum voice. He doesn't answer. He asks if she can meet him at the deli, early, so they will have the place to themselves. Of course she can. Eleven-thirty is perfect, *cheri.*

He is sitting at a table by a window. Though he's been gone only a week, his black hair is longer than she remembers, his skin a richer olive. She stands for a minute watching his fingers play with a plastic spoon. She crosses the room and sits down opposite him. His hands immediately fold over hers, so hot they scald. She jumps and he takes his hands away.

He says, "What can I get you, my love?"

His Alabama accent is softer, thicker than she remembers. Alexandra feels the prick of a tiny knife near her heart. What will she do if she loses him? While he's getting the coffee, she looks out at the street. Water from an early morning rain lies in pools on the pavement and a soft mist rises from them, giving the street a strange abstract beauty, all varying tones of gray except for a splash of pink where the water reflects a neon sign.

When he sets the cup down in front of her, he touches her shoulder. "It's so *good* to see you."

She nods. He sits, picks up his spoon.

"Tell me, how is Tom?"

"It's taken a toll."

He looks out at the street. "If I'd known this would happen—" he begins, then stops.

"If you'd known, then what?"

"Nothing. I don't know."

She leans across the table toward him. "In a moment of lunacy, I actually wondered if you wrote that letter."

"Good god, Alexandra. Good god," he repeats, as though they are the only words he knows.

"Don't worry. I know it wasn't you."

"You know—?"

"Paige," she says.

"That child? She's my slave."

"Your *what?*"

"I mean she does what I tell her. Paige isn't too swift."

"Paige," Alexandra says, slowly, distinctly, "is in love with you."

"Ahhhh, Alexandra—"

"I've watched her at openings. I've seen the way she looks at you. I know."

"You've got it wrong," Mead says and scowls.

They are quarreling. It's their first time. It is horrible—also thrilling. They sit without speaking. Finally, he says, "Alexandra, I'm afraid—"

He fiddles with the spoon.

She feels a cold mist falling, sinking into every pore.

"Fine," she says. "Go."

He stands up. It seems to her that his face is gray now, like the street. He comes and bends and kisses her cheek. Then he leaves. Through the window she watches him walk away, splashing through the sidewalk puddles. Halfway to the corner, he stops, stares down at his wet shoes and slowly shakes his head, as though reproving his feet for taking him through water.

The next day, she stays at her office until six, then phones the Obelisk. "Mr. Latourette has left for the day," Paige simpers, pretending not to recognize Alexandra. "Is there a message?"

Alexandra replaces the receiver, picks it up again.

"Hello?" Franny says. In the background, one of the daughters is playing the piano. Alexandra recognizes a scale exercise she used to hate.

"Hello? Hello? Who is this?"

Who indeed? A person who makes hang-up calls.

Mead doesn't phone the next week, or the next. It's been a month since the letter clanked into their hall. Meanwhile, she and Tommy have returned to a more or less normal life. They no longer talk about the letter. She doesn't know where the letter is. Tommy must have put it away: *saving the evidence.* Thus, she is completely unprepared when he announces one night as they are eating herbed chicken he has perfectly grilled, "I'm gonna call the fellow."

"Call—?"

"Latourette. Why shouldn't he know about the damn letter, after all we've been through?"

"He does know. I called him." She says this coolly, the words slipping from her mouth as though by magic, like pieces of silver.

"Oh?" A wide-eyed look of surprise, followed by a deep frown of suspicion. "When?"

"A week or so after the letter came. We didn't talk long. There wasn't much to say. He sounded completely shocked."

"That's all he was? Shocked?"

"The point is he obviously knew nothing about it."

"Why didn't you tell me you'd talked to him?"

"Because I'd found out nothing. Tommy," she's suddenly shouting, "*I am not having an affair with Mead Latourette. Do you want me to put it in writing? Have it notarized?*"

He gets up and comes and puts his arms around her. "Don't you want to know who wrote the thing?" he asks, an un-Tommy-like note of doubt creeping into his voice.

She hesitates. Some wayward impulse whispers that she should tell Tommy the truth. Then he will divorce her and she will be alone. Solitude is what she yearns for now.

"I'll clean up," Tommy says and gives her shoulder a little pat, not quite as gentle as it might have been. "Why don't you go out in the garden before it gets dark?"

She stands among her flowers, breathing deeply. The peonies are in full bloom, except for a few buds that haven't opened yet, that are still encrusted with ants. She bends and takes one of the buds in her hand. She wonders what Mead is doing now. Putting his daughters to bed? Helping Franny wash up from dinner? She is not jealous, just miserable. And how unfair that she and Tommy have borne the brunt of all this, that Paige has gone unpunished. What if Franny received a letter, not a vicious one, just a note. *You may be interested to know that your husband*—Alexandra feels a pleasurable tingle in her chest. She will mail the letter tomorrow. In a few days, Mead will call to tell her the awful thing that Paige has done. *Again.* She will soothe him. She's been through this, after all. They will have to talk. Of course she can meet him. Surely he will call. She looks down at the peony bud and sees that she has brushed all the ants off. Now it is clean and virginal and will never bloom.

Mead does not call. The peonies fade, shedding their petals like snow. The roses and lilies have their flagrant season, turn yellow, and die. It is September when Tommy vaults into their kitchen wielding an enormous bunch of cellophane-wrapped tulips, red, purple, white, dozens of tulips, which must have cost the earth; it is not tulip season.

"I've been an asshole," he declares.

Alexandra smiles faintly, puts the flowers in the sink, goes to the refrigerator, and takes out a bottle of a good Sancerre—she is drinking a good deal these days—opens the wine, pours.

"Cheers," she says, handing him his glass.

Tommy says, "Let's take this out on the deck."

Her neck prickles. She has told him a thousand times it's not a deck, it's a terrace. But she just turns and goes out.

They sit side by side in wrought-iron chairs.

"You have every right to divorce me," he begins.

She starts at the word *divorce.*

"I went for the whole shit-bag. I couldn't get that letter out of my mind. I remembered times you said you were too tired and I thought, oh hell, you must have been with that guy."

She sighs, drinks. So he did believe the letter. She should have confessed in the beginning, when the letter first came. They would be separated by now. She would be living in an apartment (she envisions one of those new condos near the museum), eating supper by herself, reading a novel at the table while she eats. Oh bliss.

"This gets weird," he says. "I'd look out the window and see you in the garden and imagine you were thinking about this guy. I'd say, 'You're fucking him, aren't you, babe?' I'd say it out loud, real ugly."

He slides off his chair and kneels and lays his head on her lap. She looks down at his pale red hair, as fine as a baby's, so unlike Mead's coarse dark curls.

"There's more. Jesus, how can I tell you this? I met this woman at the club."

"Met—?" she says. "Who?"

"She works in the pro shop." His voice sounds congested with misery. "We had a kind of thing this summer. Beers and laughs. OK, some fooling around."

She stares at a coppery curl near his ear. Probably she should be angry, but instead, she feels nothing. Tommy goes on talking. He's behaved like an idiot. He'll never cheat on her again.

But Alexandra is barely listening. She is imagining a scene, the way she's been doing often lately, several times a day in fact, in which she and Mead walk, hand in hand, in a part of the city she doesn't know. Yellow leaves drift across the sidewalk. She imagines saying to Mead, *You won't believe what Tommy's been up to.*

Tommy is still talking. The letter's history as far as he's concerned. He doesn't give a damn who wrote it, though he's pretty sure it was somebody who got the shaft at the firm. They're lucky the s.o.b. didn't storm the office with a loaded gun. *We're getting along better,* she imagines telling Mead. *We're looking for a new boat.*

"Can you forgive me?" Tommy's arms are looped around her waist, his head is raised hopefully.

Alexandra gazes over Tommy's head at the garden, which is messy, almost ugly. Another scene forces its way into her mind: Mead in his kitchen staring white-faced at the paper he holds. *You may be interested to know that your husband is having an affair*—Franny is sobbing, her hands covering her face. The little girls run in and they, too, begin to cry. Mead opens his fingers and lets the paper fall, shiny paper bought at Staples; Alexandra still has the rest of the pack on her desk.

She looks down at her husband, remembering what he has confessed, what he has promised. She believes he is sincere, though it will not surprise her if later he resumes the affair with the girl in the pro shop, or some other girl, and spends more time at the club with his men friends. Theirs will be that kind of marriage now. *All this is your own fault. You are selfish,*

Alexandra. It is her mother's voice coming from somewhere near the peonies. She hates those flowers now. She will dig them up, get rid of them. How could she have loved them so? How could she?

What We Do for Love

❧

"People kill each other all the time for love," Tanner tells us. She doesn't mean on TV. A few months ago, one of our local bluebloods, Tully Lassiter, found his wife *in flagrante* with the head groom in his stableful of thoroughbreds. Tully was carrying a gun. That was the end of Anne Marie Lassiter and Shep Crowder, our old high-school buddy.

Jack says, "Tully didn't shoot 'em for love. People do other things for love."

"Like what?" Tanner wants to know. "Such as?"

Her sneakers beat a tattoo on their porch floor. We're sitting out here watching the traffic and drinking beer, using coffee mugs in case Tanner's mother, who's a born-again, drives by.

"Come on, hot shot. What do people do for love?"

Jack just looks at her. They've been married eleven years. The answer could be tricky. He shifts his hard blue gaze to me. I know what he's thinking: *Weigh in, Linda baby. Solve this conundrum. Set us straight.*

They're both looking at me now.

"Don't look at me," I say. "I'm a weaver, not a shrink."

I am a weaver. Jack trains thin, nervous million-dollar mares. Tanner gives perms and plays with her tarot, trying to spy on the future. We all three turn thirty this year. Tanner looks the same as she did in high school, sharp little face, bony dancer's legs, hair cut in a pixie with a rat tail. Jack is thinner, harder than he used to be. I've put on a few pounds.

I live alone. My parents died ten years ago in a two-car crash with teenagers on the Wardensville Road. Eight dead in all. I was up at Sharpsburg State at the time, studying to be a vet. I am big and strong and my folks thought that with all the horse farms around Winslow my future would be secure. But I came home for the funeral and never went back to Sharpsburg. I started weaving instead.

Tanner says the cards indicate I will leave again when the right man comes along. She's bent on finding him.

Meanwhile, we are locked onto the local drama like everybody else: the love triangle, the murder, the trial. It's in the papers as far away as Washington, D.C., how the scion of a well-known Virginia family was arrested for killing his wife, a Firestone heiress, and her cowboy lover. Cowboy lover! Poor Shep. People start lining up outside the courthouse at six in the morning on days when something good is expected: a new witness, photographs. One of the courtroom guards is a linebacker we knew at Winslow High and he slips Tanner and me in. Jack wouldn't be caught dead at that circus, quote unquote.

What has come out at the trial is that Tully walked down to the stables and found Anne Marie and Shep in the tack room on a blanket on the floor, naked.

"In November," Tanner groans when we tell Jack this bit. "She must of froze her titties off."

I am not so sure Anne Marie was cold.

Tully's lawyers are asking for temporary insanity and probation. They claim he never knew a thing about his wife and Shep until the fatal day, even though the two of them had been visiting the tack room since August, if you believe the prosecution witnesses. The prosecutor contends that Tully planned the murder. Why else show up at the barn with a loaded twelve-gauge?

"He knew," Jack says, tipping back his I ♥ VIRGINIA mug. "You had to be blind not to know about those two. All that crowd knew and nobody gave a damn."

Jack has nothing but disrespect for the people he works for, mostly out-of-staters who have bought up the horse farms around Winslow. "They all give you the eye," he says. "The women give you the eye. Hell, the men give you the eye, too. You get your butt pinched if you don't keep moving."

Money is the other thing they like. Last year, one of the horses Jack trained won big at Palm Beach. The owner, a stockbroker from New Jersey, who is not much older than we are, built a new glass-and-redwood house up on Saddleback Ridge, nine bedrooms and a Jacuzzi. Jack and Tanner netted a Subaru.

Jack says he wouldn't be surprised if Tully set the whole thing up between Shep and Anne Marie. Tully stands to gain about eighty million.

At the trial, Tully sits impassively. He makes no gesture, does not speak. His face is creased like old leather. His hair falls in silver waves over his high taut forehead. He wears an olive shirt with an open collar and a tweed jacket woven of threads the colors of sand and gravel. He is in his forties but looks sixty. Mostly, though, Tully looks bored. Once during a break, he pulled out a paperback and started to read, but his lawyer spoke to him and he put it away.

Tully's mother, Mrs. Celia Lassiter, sits in a spectator's chair behind the defense table. She wears pearls and a pale wool suit, though it is April; the lilac and the crab apple are in bloom. Mrs. Celia Lassiter looks as though she thinks she is in church.

The prosecutor, Nancy Slade, is a no-nonsense woman with a blond pageboy and tinted glasses. She's local, but not one of the horse crowd. Tanner and I were in court the day she showed the jury the photographs of the bodies. From a distance, the images were just shapes and shadows with two small pale dispersing moons, their faces I suppose. I didn't want a better view. The white walls of the tack room were said to have been splashed bright red. But when I think of the scene, which I can't help doing, I see Anne Marie and Shep lying peacefully entwined as though they were sleeping. I'd like to think they were happy.

Tully didn't look at the pictures or look away from them. He just sat there.

"Like a zombie," Tanner whispered. "A killer zombie."

Or just bored.

Anne Marie's sister from Connecticut attends the trial every day. She looks exactly like Anne Marie except that her hair is moussed. Anne Marie wore her hair straight with a barrette on the side like a little girl, a little rich girl. She was why the Lassiters, whose money dribbled away years ago, were able to hang on to their stables, not to mention redo their house, put in a pool, hire Shep. Thanks to Anne Marie, the Lassiter farm is now a showplace. The old brick farmhouse we used to think was spooked was featured in *Southern Living* last year; the writer raved about the mantels, the moldings, Anne Marie's knot garden–beds of thyme and rosemary and lavender laid out in overlapping wheels. The stables are a quarter mile behind the house, down a gravel road lined with giant boxwood. Beyond the stables are the practice rings and beyond them, pastures so brightly green that on sunny days they make you blink. Over it all looms the gaunt blue face of Stone Man Mountain.

I knew Anne Marie slightly. She used to drop by my studio once in a while. She was a nice woman, small, with a square face and little haunted eyes. Often she lingered as though she didn't have much else to do. Her first purchase was one of my angora shawls in mauve.

She asked me once how I came to be a weaver. I don't remember anyone else ever asking me that. I know I've never tried to explain about my weaving, how I close my eyes before I take up the shuttle and think a single word—autumn or melody or wind—and then begin to weave. The colors that form on my loom are not gray or tangerine or blue, but peace or memory or desire. The pink wool for Tanner's sweater last year was the baby she and Jack got married for, then lost. Or maybe it is the next baby who is reluctant to come. Of course I did not get into all this with Anne Marie.

"I was lonesome," I told her. "My folks had just died. I set up a loom in the kitchen for company."

Her mauve eyes blinked and she said, "I see," though I don't think she did.

The last time she came, she bought one of my men's sweaters in a chestnut wool. The word I had been thinking when I wove it was warm.

"You should be very proud of your work, Linda," she said. "Your sweaters can stand up beside anybody's."

"It's so pretty," she kept saying, moving her hand over the wool. "So soft."

I thought the sweater was for Tully. I should have known that chestnut color was perfect for Shep Crowder.

Sometimes, early in the morning, Jack drops Tanner off at my place on his way to the farm where he works. I live eight miles outside Winslow, on the other side of Stone Man. People are always asking me how I get along out there by myself. Even Tanner asks me that. She likes my workroom, though, even if it used to be a garage. She says it smells nice, like dry leaves. It's cold, I remind her. The insulation isn't right. Last winter my wool froze.

Today is chilly and both of us are wearing sweaters I made. Tanner's is of a fine blue merino, cut on the bias so she will not look as though she is drowning in wool. Mine is looser, since I am so tall and big-boned. The sweaters I fashion for myself are thick and bulky, of fawn and wheat-colored wools. The one today is a reddish gold, nearly the color of my hair.

While we shove skeins into pigeonholes behind the loom, she tells me her dream.

"I was in this enormous room with wooden horses whirling around like a merry-go-round."

"That's the craft show," I say, meaning the one in Baltimore last week. I told Tanner about it after I got back. The Civic Center was lined with booths made of pinewood you could smell and people walked past the booths all day looking at the crafts, round and round and round.

"Wait," she says. "There was a love interest in my dream. He was riding a horse with a silver mane. Every time he went past, we had this tremendous attraction toward each other."

She spreads her arms and starts swinging her hips and rotating her pelvis, the way she used to do leading cheers at Winslow High. When I stop laughing, I say, "You got that right, too."

But I am thinking, *How does she know?* I didn't say a word about the furniture maker who had the booth next to mine. He and I got friendly during the show and on the last night, after all my sweaters and rugs and his stools and cane chairs were packed away, we had a few beers together.

Now my best friend is dreaming my life.

"He makes bedposts down in North Carolina," I say. "Works mostly in walnut."

"Can you beat that?" Tanner is grinning and tap-dancing fast all over the studio. "Oh boy. I'm jealous."

"Sure you are," I say.

"If I was single, I'd be outta here like that." She snaps her fingers to show how quick she would be somewhere else if she weren't married to Jack. Then she stops dancing and looks out the window. The fog has lifted off Stone Man and beyond it, down the valley, other mountains are visible, a sea of mountains wrapped in purple mist.

"North Carolina's down there," she says with a little sigh.

"Tell me one thing, Tanner," I say, slinging an arm around her shoulders. "In your dream, did that love interest ever get off the merry-go-round?"

Tanner shakes her head. "I guess I woke up too soon."

Then we both burst out laughing.

When Tanner and I were in the ninth grade, we used to call Shep Crowder on the phone and hang up when he said hello. Then we'd die laughing, roll around on the floor like the idiots we were in those days. We've been best friends since we were seven and spent second grade pretending we were twins. The year we turned thirteen, Tanner's mother went God crazy and Tanner moved out to live with us until her mother calmed down enough to let her wear lipstick. Even in adolescence we never became un-twinned.

Shep was a big tawny boy, not very smart but sweet, a little vain. His father ran a garage and his mother helped out at a day-care center. Both his parents were small pale people and there was Shep, flaxen-haired, over six feet tall, all Technicolor. Tanner liked the way his yellow boots matched his hair. She looks dumbfounded whenever I remind her of this.

"You had a crush on Shep a mile wide," I like to tell her. "You thought he looked like Bo on *The Dukes of Hazzard.*"

"Me? You're the one, Linda," she'll insist. "You always wanted to ride by Shep's house and honk."

"Easy, girls," Jack says when we get going. But he loves to hear us wrangle.

We didn't meet Jack until senior year when he moved into Winslow from Poolesville to live with his grandparents. His mother had married the man who ran the Poolesville gas station and Jack and the stepdad didn't get along.

We spotted him one day eating alone in the cafeteria. His black hair reached his shoulders. His thin face told you nothing.

"Double dare," Tanner said and we marched our trays over to his table.

"We saw you looking," Tanner told him.

"Looking at who?" Jack asked and stared at me so hard I forgot to breathe. I was a big girl even then, but for a second I felt so light I thought I'd float up to the ceiling.

Tanner snorted and we both sat down.

After that, Jack and Tanner and I made a threesome. During breaks at school, we stood together in the halls watching the other kids watching other kids or sat out in the parking lot while Jack smoked. On weekends we rode around in Tanner's daddy's Eldorado, the three of us scrunched together in the front seat, Tanner driving, Jack in the middle. We'd pull into the Dairy Queen and sit there eating vanilla cones and listening to WLOV, The Best Countre-e-e. Nobody knew which of us Jack liked better, though most people probably picked Tanner. She was half my size and a cheerleader. Somehow, though, I always thought it was me.

A week before graduation, Tanner and I were trying on white dresses in a stamp-size Penney's dressing room when she said in a sad little voice, "Linda, nothing's gonna fit," and lifted a lacy skirt to let me see her tummy.

All I could think to say was, "Who?" Of course I should have known.

It is a time I don't think about much anymore, but when I do, each detail gleams like fresh paint in my mind: the two of us sitting on the floor in that little white room among piles of crushed cotton and eyelet embroidery, Tanner in the too-tight lace, me in a shapeless thing with a big collar that didn't suit me at all but which I ended up graduating in. I remember my large face in the mirror, shining with sweat, surprisingly calm. Tanner didn't have to tell me she was going to go ahead and have the baby.

"Jack won't talk," she said. "He just stares off in space. Like a zombie."

Then she broke down crying. It was all I could do to get her out of the lace and the room.

I took her home, then I drove to Jack's. He must have been watching for me because he came out of the house even before I stopped the car. He didn't look at me, just got in and nodded toward the windshield as though he wanted me to drive, so I did. The sun had just gone down; the sky was the thick yellow-white of buttermilk. We were almost to Pigeon Run when he said, "I can't stand this. Stop somewhere." I pulled off into a stand of poplars where fishermen park near the river. At first he just sat there, shoulders hunched, staring at the dark trees. Finally he said, "It ain't what you're thinking, Linda."

"I'm not thinking anything," I said.

"It happened that weekend you were off with your parents."

"It only takes once." I knew I sounded bitter.

He was silent. Then he said, "What can I do?"

He'd been planning to go to Tennessee to learn to be a big-time trainer. He already knew more about horses than anybody else around Winslow.

I said, "A baby needs two parents."

"I know that," he said. "I ain't going anywhere. It's you."

I tried to breathe. After a while, I said, "I'll be all right, Jack. We all will." My voice sounded as though I was at the end of a tunnel. I had never heard that voice before and haven't since.

He reached out then and took my hand. There wasn't a moon and the dark closed thick as curtains around us. We stayed there in the poplars for a long time. By the time we drove back to town, I felt, not better, but different.

Jack and Tanner got married up in Harrisburg the day after graduation, just the two of them and a justice of the peace. Not long after that, she lost the baby. She hasn't been able to get pregnant since. Her mother says it's the judgment of God. Tanner calls it the revenge of the womb, when she mentions it, which isn't often anymore. She is fragile, though, under all her talk. Jack and I both know it. Which is why things stay as they are I guess. He has his horses. Tanner keeps busy with her cards. I weave.

Since Palm Beach, the stockbroker has taken to calling Jack "my man." "Here's my man," he says when he brings his guests from New Jersey down to his stables to admire his horses. The guests pile out of his Jeep, half-tanked, dressed the way they must imagine people in the country dress, in silk shirts, designer jeans, Hermés scarves. The women brighten when they see Jack in his soft fawn jodhpurs and boots. He's about my height, razor thin, with a cowlick that flips his dark hair over his forehead. But Jack has eyes only for Cindy, his prizewinner, jet black, all muscle and bone. The guests don't make a sound as he mounts her and rides her down to the far ring, elbows tight, hands low, steady as rain.

He is there today when Tanner and I stop by the farm on our way into town to check out the trial. I pull the Honda up next to the barn. From our distance, horse and rider look like toy figures, as though somebody has wound them up: round and round and round.

"I expected Dwayne might be here," Tanner says and slides me a look.

Dwayne is the other trainer at the farm, a huge man with a red beard. Dwayne's favorite thing, next to horses, is hunting. He has brought me quail and pheasant and deer and, once, some bear meat I threw away.

"We could wait," Tanner says, meaning for Dwayne.

I don't say anything. I am looking at Jack and Cindy moving together like slow dancers locked in their own rhythm, which is the way I feel when I am at my loom, the only sound the tiny hum the threads make as the shuttle moves back and forth, back and forth.

"I don't know why you stay around here," Tanner says.

"I've told you," I say. "I like the colors. Every shade of green on the planet's right here."

I start the car. We both take a last look at the far ring.

"Jack dreams about that horse," Tanner says as we drive off. "In his sleep he'll go, *Easy, girl, easy,* and moan."

In the courtroom, Tully sits stone-faced as Nancy Slade describes how calmly and deliberately he loaded his gun and walked down the boxwood drive from the house to the stables. How in the dusty barn with its scented shadows, its snuffle of horses' breath, its pregnant air, he opened the door of the tack room.

"The defendant had to know they would be there, ladies and gentlemen. They met at the stable every Thursday afternoon and had been doing so for three months, since Mr. Lassiter began seeing a chiropractor in Winslow on that day. Only, this Thursday, he parked his Mercedes out on the road and walked back to the house. He went into the house and took his gun from the rack in his study where he kept it, and then, ladies and gentlemen, he loaded the gun. He walked down to the barn carrying a loaded gun in order to kill his wife and her lover."

I try to imagine Tully as he walked. Was he looking up at Stone Man's familiar old mug? Did he notice the bright green pastures with their new white fences and admire Anne Marie's herb garden? Or did he see only his own cold breath hanging in the air?

"The defense suggests he took his gun to the stable to clean it. To clean a loaded gun? The evidence is quite clear, ladies and gentlemen, that the defendant never cleaned his guns in the barn. He always cleaned them at the house. Furthermore, we have testimony that the defendant's guns had all been cleaned that very week by the defendant himself and Mr. Crowder."

She has already shown that the defendant enjoyed Mr. Crowder's company, cleaning guns, taking the dogs for a run, visiting the local tavern. She has shown that the defendant had recently made Mr. Crowder the gift of a new Isuzu Trooper. *Draw your own conclusions, ladies and gentlemen,* and a lot of people have. Poor Shep.

For her final admonition, the prosecutor walks over and stands directly in front of the jury. "Ladies and gentlemen, whatever the error committed by the defendant's wife and Shep Crowder, however grievously wrong you may consider their conduct to have been, it did not give Tully Lassiter the right to end their lives in a pool of blood on a stable floor."

She sits down, takes her glasses off, and wipes the lenses on her sleeve. The jury looks dazed. Tanner whispers, "He's cooked."

But now Tully's lawyer stands up. He is an old friend of Tully's from Woodbury Forest, the tony prep school where all our so-called scions get ready for life. Right away, he takes the jury into his confidence, explaining in a deep soothing voice how dearly Tully loved his wife, how solid their marriage was, childless but full of shared interests like horses and dogs and—

"Shep Crowder?" someone yells in the back of the room. Tanner and I swivel to see who the mouth belongs to. A man we don't recognize is being escorted out by our friend, the linebacker. The judge taps his hammer and the titters subside. The lawyer pours himself a glass of water.

The windows of the courtroom are open and the odor of lilac pours in. On Mrs. Celia Lassiter's face is a little smile she has probably forgotten. It makes her look expectant, as though any minute we are all going to stand up and sing a hymn. Suddenly, there is murmuring in the courtroom. I notice that Tully's shoulders are heaving spasmodically. His mother reaches out a hand but doesn't touch him.

"Sweet Jesus," Tanner whispers. "Is he having a heart attack?"

I say, "I think he's crying."

"The guy should be in Hollywood," Jack says. "Who does Tully think he's fooling?"

He gets up and goes to get another beer. We're in their living room; Tanner invited me to dinner after the court finished. She looks at me and shrugs. Nobody knows why Tully started with the tears. The linebacker told us at the break that he kept asking his lawyer about his dogs. "Who's feeding them, Phil? Dammit, man, who's feeding the *dogs?*"

Jack comes back with a Rolling Rock. "Make room, girls," he says and sits down on the sofa between us. "What else's new?"

Tanner says, "Linda has a new interest. From North Carolina."

"Linda got a new man?" Jack puts one arm around Tanner and the other around me and hugs us both. "Let's make him jealous."

It's Jack who should be in Hollywood, I think. Tanner swats him on the back of the head.

"Linda found him up in Baltimore and I dreamed him. He works in wood."

Nobody says anything.

Finally Jack asks, "What's for din-din?"

"Chops. Can't you smell 'em?" Tanner jumps up and performs a two-step jitterbug, starting into one of her cheerleader routines.

"Gimme a N!" she shouts.

What is she up to? But Jack and I are used to this. Obediently, we roar, "N!"

"Gimme a O!"

"O!"

"Gimme a R!"

"R!"

We spell it out and all three of us scream in unison, "North Carolina! North Carolina! North Carolina!"

The room is deadly quiet when we finish, like the courtroom when one of the lawyers sits down. Then Tanner says in her normal voice, "I'll do you a reading after dinner, Linda," and goes off to the kitchen.

I think about the reading: *Will Linda pursue the North Carolina interest? Will Linda leave Winslow? Who does Linda love?*

I try to remember the furniture maker at the Baltimore show, to resurrect the color of his eyes, the shape of his mouth, his name. Tanner is right: I ought to leave. Is it crazy to think that if I go, their baby will come? I look at Jack, who is nursing his beer, brooding on something, probably Cindy. Then I make a gigantic effort and recall the furniture maker's hands, long and pale and unusually smooth for someone in his line of work. Before I can conjure anything else, Tanner is calling, "Food's on, you all."

At dinner, we can't shut up about the trial.

"Okay," Tanner says, "the defense says Tully's out of his mind when he pulls the trigger. But an hour later, he's sitting at his kitchen table working the crossword. What's that supposed to mean?"

That is what Tully was doing when the sheriff found him, after Tully phoned his mother and his mother phoned the lawyer who phoned the law. The gun was propped against the stove.

Jack shakes his head. "Those people. What's for dessert?"

"Nothing you like." Tanner hops up. "Uh-uh," she says when I start to help, so I sit back down. She heads into the kitchen with our dishes.

Right away I see the stain on the tablecloth. The cloth is pale blue. I made it about a year after I started weaving, and it's the one that convinced me I could be a good weaver. The stain is in the middle, so we can't tell who made it. It could have been any of us.

Jack's eyes follow mine. "Damn," he says.

We both reach out at the same time to rub the spot. Our hands hit each other instead. We draw back, then I reach out and scratch at the spot, then Jack does, our fingers dancing around each other so as not to touch. But it doesn't do any good. The stain doesn't budge. It's probably pork grease.

"Mighty quiet in there," Tanner yells from the kitchen. "Can't you all think of anything to talk about when I'm not around?"

"We're talking about you," Jack yells back. "In sign language."

I dip my napkin into my water glass and rub, but it just makes a darker spot.

"You really got something goin' down in North Carolina?" Jack asks.

"I don't think it's going to come out," I say.

"Huh, Linda?"

I feel like crying. I can't stand seeing that stain on the cloth. "Soda might do it," I say. "Or Borax."

"Is he worth it, Linda? What's he like?"

I'm afraid of making it worse by rubbing it. I try to remember what you're supposed to use on grease.

Jack whispers, "Don't go, Linda."

I look at him then. Our hands snake out and into each other. I feel the familiar calluses on his palms.

"I'm not going anywhere," I say.

He sighs. Our hands release. He picks up the sugar bowl and puts it down on top of the stain. The blue cloth is flawless again, a soft pure blue like the sky after a summer rain. Then *bam!* The kitchen door bangs and I let out a shriek. Tanner is there, balancing three plates of hot pie. I'm holding my hands out in front of me like a shield. They both look at me as though I'm loony tunes.

Tully is no longer bored. Today he wears a tan shirt with the sand-and-gravel jacket. He sits straight, legs crossed, tapping a finger on the table and studying the prosecutor, the judge, his lawyer, though none of them is doing anything, saying anything. Occasionally, he nods as though he has come to some conclusion, like the jury who are expected to return any minute now. Once, he rotates, looks back, and frowns, as though he's surprised to find all of us sitting here. His eyes scan our faces. You can see him thinking, *Who are these people?*

Tanner pokes me. The jurors are filing back in. Then everything speeds up like a video on fast forward. The judge asks the foreman to stand up; a bearded man in a dark suit does. And then we know. Tully doesn't move a muscle, though his lawyer is whispering to him. The prosecutor smiles and takes off her glasses. Mrs. Celia Lassiter stares at nothing. She no longer looks as though she knows where she is. Suddenly, I am filled with grief. I remember Anne Marie and her little haunted eyes and the way she touched my chestnut wool, so full of longing. "Warm," I think. She and Shep shouldn't be dead.

"You okay?" Tanner whispers.

I take a deep breath and nod.

We're hardly out of the courthouse when Tanner announces that she's getting back to my future, now that we pretty well know Tully's.

"North Carolina's not that far," she says. "We'll visit."

I lean down and give her a hug. She hugs me back, her bony little arms digging into my shoulders.

"Stop worrying about me," I tell her, the way I always do when she tries to manage my life.

Maybe one day I will leave. People do all sorts of things for love.

"Come to the house," she says. "I'll do you a reading."

I shake my head. I'm headed home. Jack's birthday is soon. I am planning a sweater for him that will be the color of the mountains I see from my window when the fog lifts, a sea of mountains wrapped in purple mist. I will thread the loom, knot the warp, and begin my slow dance with the shuttle. I will think as I weave, Stone Man.

The Obi Tree

✑

"A little to the left," Bobbi says.

She is lying on their bed while John massages her long narrow back. He moves to the left, she gives a little cry, he smiles. It
reminds him of the sounds she used to make when they made
love.

"How's that, ma'am?"

"Good," she says.

She is not wearing her wig. Her head, perfectly oval, is covered with a soft brown fuzz. He has come to think she is most
beautiful this way, though Bobbi says she looks like something
out of *Star Trek*.

She turns over and stretches out her long legs, her feet with
their scarlet toenails. John painted the nails yesterday, spending
more than an hour getting them right.

"Maybe you can get something done on your thesis," she
says.

He lies down beside her. He too is very long and lean; the
two of them are almost identical lengths. John is blond, his hair

fine and long, touching his shoulders. Bobbi says, "John wears the hair in this house."

Now he frowns. He does not know what she wants for this day. They have planned nothing. He blames himself for leaving it up in the air.

"Do your trick, John," she says.

But he doesn't reply. He props his arms behind his head and stares out the window at the tree. Neither John nor Bobbi knows what kind of tree this is that fills their bedroom window. For them, it has no name, only a presence. Now, in the middle of a white North Carolina spring, the branches of this beautiful tree explode with dark purple buds as intricate and tight as the folds of a Japanese *obi*.

"Come on." She nudges him with her elbow, which is sharp, nearly fleshless, and causes pain like water near his heart. "Do your trick."

"Ouch."

"Well, do it."

He slides his hands from behind his head and cups them over his mouth. He begins to yodel, a bottled, alarming sound that creates in his mind the image of a distant mountain peak, colored in unreal blues and greens, like an old ad for a menthol cigarette.

Bobbi giggles: her giggles, his yodels. Now she begins to laugh, a helpless hiccuping sound, and he stops.

He puts his arm under her head. She is still laughing, but soundlessly, shaking as though a vibrator has gotten hold of her, little tremors scurrying all over her body. He looks down at her head, at the smudged purplish line that whimsically encircles it.

Abruptly she stops laughing, and he thinks she has fallen asleep. Sometimes she does that; all of a sudden, they will be talking and then—she sleeps because of the medication. Most days, she does not wake up until noon. Then he brings in her orange juice and lies down beside her while she drinks it, and they watch the tree.

Bobbi says, "Which wig will it be today, John?"

So she isn't asleep. Instead, it is John who feels drowsy, his eyelids heavy as though pressed by pennies. He knows he is not really sleepy, that he is attempting to feel as she does, to assume the state of her mind. He forces open his eyes and tries to think about wigs.

Bobbi's wigs. Blond, brunette, auburn. Short, long, curly, straight. Bobbi's wigs are all styles, all shades, all expensive. The wigs rankle John's mother, who asks, "What's the use of her fixing herself up when—?" But Bobbi herself is clear about the wigs. "I'm living fast," she says and grins.

It is Bobbi's father, Theo, fat owner of a trucking company, who buys the wigs. Theo buys Bobbi whatever she wants. Each time he visits, he appeals to her to ask him for something. His hand hovers at his wallet pocket. "Please, honey," he says, "wha'chya need?" Bobbi needs nothing but always asks for something: a new camera, sunlamp, golf lessons. She is shameless about asking.

"Wear the long straight one," John says.

"The coed coif?"

"Yea-a-ah."

"John, you are so sentimental I can't stand it."

The long straight-hair wig—he thinks of it as a sorrel color—reminds him of Bobbi as she looked when he met her at the university junior year, when she became his girl. He still thinks of her that way sometimes, his girl, though they have been married for nearly five years.

"It was your mind I loved," Bobbi has told him. (They often recall this period.) "I loved talking to you, John."

But his memories are almost entirely sexual—Bobbi sitting on his bed reading Marvell aloud, cross-legged, wearing a bulky sweater and nothing else; Bobbi beneath him in the backseat of his freezing Oldsmobile, her head on a volume of eighteenth-century prose, her breasts a lavish green in the light of the street lamp; Bobbi standing naked in his bedroom while he lifts her breasts, small and soft, in his hands. He has never told her of these memories, though he thinks he probably should.

"Okay. I'm hopelessly sentimental. That's the way I am."

"That's all right." She giggles. "I'm hungry."

He sits up, alert. Food is a topic of terrible interest to him. He thinks endlessly about what Bobbi will eat, what he will be able to fix.

"Jell-O?" he says.

She groans.

"Cereal? We've got Grape-Nuts."

She groans louder and pretends to vomit.

"Okay. Frozen chicken pot pie."

"Soup," she says. "Have we got soup?"

"Sure we have soup," he says, trying to remember. "I think we have soup. Maybe tomato."

"Chicken noodle," she says.

If they don't have it, he will go and get it.

"With grilled cheese?" he asks.

"Yum. I'll make the sandwiches."

"Come on, Bobbi. Oh fuck."

This is their daily argument, which he nearly always loses. Bobbi is not supposed to use the kitchen knives, but she does anyway. Her fingers are jeweled with pearl-white scars. Whenever his mother visits, she takes John aside and asks, "Well, how many times has she cut herself this week? Has she chopped off a finger yet?" His mother has not been able to forgive Bobbi for having a brain tumor.

"As a favor to me—" he begins.

"I just remembered. Ivan is sending some people over this afternoon. What time is it?"

Then he too remembers what he has planned for this day— the day before Bobbi returns to the hospital for yet another operation, one that nobody believes will save her life, only prolong it, a little. He has planned that they will be totally alone today.

"No," he says and pounds a pillow.

"Three o'clock," Bobbi says. "They're coming at three."

"It's not fair," John says. "It's not fair of Ivan to ask us to see anyone today and it's not fair of you to let them come without telling me."

"I'm sorry. I forgot. They won't stay long."

"But when they leave you'll be tired. You'll go to sleep."

"John, I will go to sleep anyway."

He lies back on the bed. What she says is true. Whatever they do today, she will sleep for most of it.

Bobbi nestles up against him and begins to hum. She has never been able to carry a tune well, now not at all, but after a while he recognizes "Jude" and begins to hum it with her while they watch the fat buds of the nameless tree slowly rise and fall in the wind.

A little before three, Ivan Nicholson, the kindly, overworked head of counseling at the Duke cancer clinic, calls to say the people he was sending over can't make it after all. They will come another time, he says in a tired voice ground into a permanent whisper by the serenity he must constantly assume. Ivan is in his forties but looks much older and much sicker than the patients he tries to help.

Ivan has sat beside John for hours, days, weeks, after Bobbi's two operations. (The tumor has never grown cleanly on the surface of her brain. They have never been able to get it all.) Ivan is there even when the parents have driven away—Theo and Anna to their large, white house overlooking a golf course a hundred miles to the east, where they pray together, for hours, in large, white, plush-carpeted rooms; John's mother to her spare apartment near the university in Greensboro where her husband spent his life teaching, where she sits beside a single lamp reading Trollope and drinking a raw red Italian wine. Even then, Ivan is still there in the hospital room, huddled on one of the cracked vinyl chairs, watching John watching

Bobbi's bruised, almost vanished face. Outside the room, in the hall where they go to walk off the muscle aches and deeper cramps of their vigil, John tells Ivan to leave, just leave him alone goddammit go away get the hell *out!* But Ivan refuses to let John go through this alone, the way John would like to.

"Hold on, old man," says Ivan's gravelly voice on the telephone. "I've got an idea."

"I'm holding," says John.

It has been three years since the last operation and still Ivan is with them, as much a part of their lives as the cancer or the tree outside the bedroom window. Ivan calls. He visits. He organizes. He sends streams of patients from the clinic in Durham to their apartment in Chapel Hill. "What are we supposed to do with these people?" John demands. "Get them drunk?" But Bobbi welcomes them joyfully. She invites them to sit on their sofa, tells them how happy she is to see them, asks them questions, listens, tells them about herself, cracks jokes. She is patient, humorous, direct. She is strong, funny, wise. She assures those who are gravely ill that there are worse things in life than death, something John will never believe.

What John does on these occasions is make tea, which he brings into the living room on a tray. He serves the tea in perfect silence. With a slight inclination of his head, he indicates cream, sugar, the silver dish in which he has arranged a pinwheel of lemon slices. But he will not speak. "John is very angry about all this," Bobbi tells the startled, embarrassed guests. Then she smiles at John and nods, assuring him that his anger, his fierce possessiveness, his outrage are all right. Or rather, they are something he will get over, like chicken pox. As she has.

"Listen, buddy," Ivan says, "are you and Bobbi up for a little putt-putt this afternoon?"

"Christ, Ivan!"

Then John tells Ivan that they have plans. Right now, they are finishing their lunch—Yes, he knows it is three o'clock. Later, they plan to go out for a drive. Thanks for checking in, Ivan old buddy, Ivan old friend. John hears in his own voice the flutey, insincere note of a certain type of preacher he detests. He feels his lips stretching into a smile which Ivan cannot see. He is inexpressibly angry.

Bobbi watches from where she sits at the table behind the sofa, holding a spoon. She smiles. Her gray eyes are luminous. Her face glows with what could reasonably be mistaken for health but is actually something called "Touch and Glow," which John has applied, painstakingly, to her cheeks. Silky sorrel hair flows over her shoulders. She is wearing a crimson sweater and looks, besides healthy and beautiful, about twelve years old.

"Tell Ivan I love him," she says.

For some reason, John cannot get these words out. He understands he is angry with Ivan because he cannot be angry with Bobbi. He knows that he is not really angry with Bobbi either. He and Ivan have been over this many times. He knows that Ivan, who is possibly his best friend in the world, probably knows that at this moment John wants to scream, to curse. John gently replaces the telephone receiver.

"It's all right, John," Bobbi says.

She is still smiling, but it is as though she has forgotten to adjust her expression to what is actually happening. Her reactions are often delayed this way: she has lost the ability to synchronize, laughs long after a joke is told, or before it is finished, or goes on laughing too long. These are things John no longer notices. He realizes that to some people, Bobbi is radically altered. Her speech is slow, her movements unreliable, her face off-center as though the bones have slipped under her skin. But minute by minute, John memorizes her, so thoroughly that nothing about her can surprise him now. His attention is so complete that the changes in his wife are no more startling to him than if they had occurred naturally over many years, as they grew old together.

Now she is standing. Because she is tall, almost as tall as he is, she must bend a little to hold onto the back of the sofa.

"Let's go, John," she says, still smiling, "before your mother calls."

They drive along the roller-coaster Hillsborough Road into town, then out again on the flatter, but still winding road toward Pittsboro. They are not talking about where they are going; they just drive as though they don't care where they end up.

"Do you smell it?" Bobbi asks.

They are driving past fields of plowed black earth.

"Yea-a-ah. What is it?"

"I don't know."

What he smells is rich, almost bitter, like cheese. Perhaps it is the odor of the wet earth rotting with spring dampness. Whatever it is, it is invigorating, stirring. It inspires John with a vast sexual longing.

He rolls down the window, sticks his head out, and yodels. Bobbi screams with laughter. She loves this trick. Yodeling. He used to do it, half drunk or just being funny, to make her laugh. When they were driving somewhere, or in the mountains, or at the beach. On a motel balcony one muggy summer night, after their wedding. After her operation (the first one) when he tried to pull her, *drag* her back into consciousness.

Later, she could not remember the word.

Make those sounds, John, you know—What sounds? What do you mean, Bobbi? Frowning, fingers clenched, she strikes and strikes her bandaged head. Whistling? Singing? Darling, what sounds? Until he thinks: yodeling.

"Look," Bobbi says.

He looks but does not know what she wants him to see: the little white petals that float around in the air, the yellow forsythia beside the road, the woods deeply white with dogwood, or in the distance, over the feathered tops of trees, a mauve hill.

He turns off onto a gravel road and the car shudders over the ancient ruts. He glances at Bobbi. Though it is not cold, merely brisk, she is wrapped in a red coat. A white turban covers her head, frames her face. Faint threadlike lines are visible between her eyebrows. She is frowning, looking for something.

"Look," she says again, possibly meaning the house.

John always sees this house with surprise: he remembers it as bigger, sturdier, holier than the frail red plywood box he finds on the edge of the woods. Perhaps this is because the kudzu has not yet begun to grow. By early summer, the house will be entirely encased by this wild, thickly spreading leafy vine which, unchecked, John believes, could clothe the whole of North Carolina. Vine-bedecked, the house will seem opulent, majestic, while now it is naked, its bare sides stained an embarrassing rose.

In the yard are parked a green Volkswagen beetle, a white Corvair, and a rusty red MG, signaling the continued, perhaps permanent occupancy of this house by graduate students.

"I'll bet they're cold in there," Bobbi remarks.

"Why cold?"

In this house, John and Bobbi have made endless love. He remembers this house as though it were filled with hot steam.

"Don't you remember? We were always freezing," Bobbi says.

John looks in bewilderment at his wife. Cold in that house? Always freezing? He wonders how she remembers their love-making, whether she remembers it, whether it is only he who—but he does not ask. If he asks, she will not necessarily tell him the truth.

She reaches over and lays a hand on his knee. Its weight is that of one of the pale floating petals that adorn their windshield. He covers it with his.

"Are you cold now?"

Her hand has the coolness of something inanimate, something that does not sweat. She shakes her head, no.

They drive on, away from the house, over the hard ribbed road, past more bungalows with parking lots for front yards. The mauve hill is on their right, now, beyond fields of black nubby earth. It is an oddly bare hill; there are no houses, no trees on it, though John believes, but is not sure, that he can see a tiny figure on the crest.

"Do you see anything on that hill over there?" he asks Bobbi.

She squints in the direction he points. Her eyesight is not good. He knows she cannot see more than a purplish blur where the hill rises.

"Yes," she lies. "I think so."

In the backseat of the car, shifting from side to side as they jerk over the ruts, are the slick white and gray folders John uses in his work: he is no longer a graduate student, an Eighteenth-Century Man; he is an insurance salesman. This too was Ivan's idea. "Don't worry about the degree now," Ivan has told him. "What you need is something active." Ivan's voice is barely above a whisper. John leans forward to hear; they are conspirators. "You can also use the income."

John knows it is not really the money Ivan worries about—Bobbi's father has enough of that. It is not even John's state of mind. Ivan has turned him into a salesman in order to save Bobbi from his hovering presence, his anxiety, his demand, taut, unspoken, absolute, that she live.

"What are you thinking about?" Bobbi asks.

They have arrived at another paved road, parallel to the one they turned off before. To the left is town, to the right the bare mauve hill.

"Nothing. A little about work," he says, though this is not true. He has simply been listening to the sound of the folders sliding back and forth on the backseat. The sound is comforting. It turns out Ivan was right. John likes his work, looks forward to the moment each day—Bobbi dressed, fed, medicated—when he gets into his car and with his folders drives out seeking people who will buy insurance. As he drives, his mind begins to sharpen, to clear, to focus on this single, narrow, reachable goal. By the time he reaches the first address inscribed in his notebook, he is animated, excited; his pulse races.

He is an excellent salesman. In his khaki suit and blue shirt, with his brown eyes and blond hair, his smile, John is someone people like to invite into their homes. He realizes this, sees himself as they see him when they ask him to sit down, a tall, lanky, good-looking young man, also polite. (John's manners are old-fashioned, Southern: he stands up when a woman enters the room, holds doors. Bobbi laughs at these ways of his. Oh John, you are too funny!) "Are you a Carolina man?" inquires the prospective insured. "There's something about you Carolina men—Now what is it you're selling? Won't you have some iced tea?"

Even John has a hard time comprehending his success. All he knows is that when he is selling insurance, he forgets about everything except the necessity of persuading whoever he is sitting across from that the best investment they can possibly make with their money is life insurance.

He turns right.

"Where are we going?" Bobbi wants to know.

Their usual route is left: back into town, past the Bell Tower, Old Quad, library, English building, arboretum, bookshop on Franklin Street—a journey they have made hundreds of times. But today, John turns right, toward the hill.

He is still listening to the shifting folders. What does the sound remind him of? Sand? Tides? Actually, the folders remind him that he has not worked in over a month now, since Bobbi's dreams came back.

"Where are we going?" Bobbi asks again, louder.

Bobbi's dreams are of white bathrooms whose ceilings rise immense distances above the spot where she lies huddled on a cold tile floor. Clear wounding light flows into this tall space from the ceiling, miles above, where, as she looks up, she sees John's face, distorted.

He has made her describe her dreams over and over to him because he hopes to dream them, too, as vividly as she does. But he never has. John does not dream at all, or if he does, he does not remember his dreams. When he lies down at night beside Bobbi, he is suddenly so weary he thinks he cannot move again, ever.

He says, "I thought we'd take a look at that hill."

"Okay," Bobbi says.

She leans back against the seat. John notices that the lines between her eyebrows are gone, but there are bluish shadows under her eyes. She is getting tired.

"What are you thinking about?" he asks.

She is silent, her eyes closed. No, he thinks, it is too early for you to sleep.

But then she says, in an almost clear, barely slurred voice, "I was thinking about the kudzu. I was thinking that one summer it will all die and fall off, and you know what?"

"What?" John says.

"There won't be anything underneath. The kudzu will have *eaten* the house."

Her whimsy startles John. Bobbi is usually the most literal

of persons, literal even in her beliefs, which include God and a heaven where, she will say forthrightly, charmingly, she will find her much loved grandmother.

"Come on!" John will reply.

But his disbelief does not bother Bobbi. She has read the books, understood the near-death experiences, talked endlessly with Ivan, who also includes an afterlife in his belief system. She speaks confidently of death as "a sense of light and wholeness and tremendous peace," where her grandmother (part of the light? an intenser ray?) will be waiting for her.

John does not believe any of this, or rather, does not care. What death is seems irrelevant beside what it is not. It is not life, that is enough to know. Death is something else; he pictures a blank gray wall.

But he can understand kudzu eating houses.

"I'm not *serious*, John," Bobbi says.

She is grinning at him.

"I'm making a joke, for heaven's sake."

He knows that she meant to be funny, but he cannot smile or laugh, though he wants to.

"I just don't understand—" he begins, without knowing what he will say.

Bobbi unbuckles her seat belt, slides over, lays her head on his shoulder. John puts his arm around her.

"This isn't safe," he says.

The car has bucked its way up a dwindling rocky road to the top of the hill, which is really not a very large hill, he sees, now that they are on it. They get out of the car and walk out onto a flat grassy space from where they can see the tops of hundreds of trees.

"Look at all the red," Bobbi says.

It is true, in this white spring, there is red everywhere, in the grass that covers the hill, in the patches of bare earth below, the leaf buds. And the smell of raw earth is, for John, almost overpowering.

Bobbi puts her hand in his.

"It's the perfect place," she says.

His heart lurches. "For what?"

"Your trick, John."

Yodeling. But he wants a mountain, clear and visible, toward which he can direct his voice. Here, there are no mountains, just swells of earth and trees, mostly trees.

"Wait a minute," he says.

He returns to the car and finds a blanket in the trunk, crumpled under tools, a loose tire, a warped copy of John Donne. It is an old green blanket, moldy and acrid and soft. He carries it to where Bobbi stands on this fairly level space and spreads it out on the ground.

"Madam."

She lies motionless in his arms while he touches her. First he draws his hand along her cheek, then finds her narrow shoulder under the red coat, slips his hand into the neck of the sweater. With the tips of his fingers, he traces the delicate ridge of clavicle until he reaches the soft depression in her throat that exactly fits his thumb.

"Mmmm," she says.

"Are you cold?"

"Are you kidding?"

She grins up at him, lying.

"Were you always cold then?" he asks.

"Then when?"

"In our little red house. That year."

"Oh. Not all the time."

"When weren't you?"

"John, I'm getting fuzzy. What is it you want to know?"

He leans down and kisses her mouth. She feels warm, her throat, her lips, her tongue, everywhere he touches her she feels warm. But he knows better than to believe it. The half-moons under her eyes are a dark, dark blue.

"Nothing," he says.

They have already discussed all the possibilities. The way the Japanese sometimes choose to die, he has told her, is really very beautiful. Husband and wife together. Lovers. Even, sometimes, a mother and her children. He talked softly, persuasively, in his best salesman mode. Think about it, Bobbi. Take your time. It just might be—

Always Bobbi has said, John, no.

Now his hand covers her small soft breast, feels on the surface of his palm a tiny movement of the nipple. Or he thinks he feels this.

When the time comes, John, Bobbi has said, we will both know it. It will be a relief to both of us. You will let me go.

And although John knows that this is probably true, his future acquiescence only fills him with disgust.

Gently, very gently, he lowers himself over her, keeping his weight off her with his hands, but touching her with the full length of his body. Closing his eyes, he imagines her body shattering under him, the transparent bone flying in pieces in all directions, each shard containing the tiny crimson seed of his lust.

Bobbi murmurs something, her voice muffled, indistinct. He hears her as from a distance, feels her pushing at him. He hesitates, then rolls off to the side, off the blanket onto the grass, buries his face in the grass.

Now the feathery weight of Bobbi crawls onto his back; he feels her on him like a huge, nearly weightless insect. Her bones impale him; wherever she touches him, there is pain. Her breath stings his neck.

She whispers, "John, do your trick."

John lifts his head, drags his hands to his mouth and, in this impossible position, he yodels. The primitive wordless cry careens wildly across the peaks and crevices of his voice, as though he has gone mad. He closes his eyes against this cataract of sound. Bobbi stirs on his back, but he is hardly conscious of her anymore.

He does not know how long they lie there or whether he sleeps, though he retains an impression of having dreamed. Finally, he draws a deep breath, then very gently slides his wife to the ground, picks her up without waking her, carries her to the car.

He lies on their bed looking out the window. It is dark now, but against the dull sky he can make out the branches of their *obi* tree, the spectral leaves, the intricate buds. Tired, he is nonetheless thinking of sex, of orifices and swelling softnesses and boneless hands that touch his body with the lightness of wind. He turns on his side to face a sleeping Bobbi. She is as serene and beautiful as a painting.

He thinks of calling Ivan. Or, even, calling his mother, who is still up, smoking, endlessly rereading Trollope. He does not think of calling Theo and Anna, who are, he knows, already asleep in their enormous impersonal bed, their clothes laid neatly on chairs ready for the early hour when they will rise and dress and, after praying, drive the hundred miles west to Durham. They will all meet at the hospital—Theo and Anna, John's mother, the doctors, the bright young nurses, Ivan, Ivan's troop of earnest, hopeful counselors. John's mother will whisper, "Why is everybody around here *smiling*?"

The scene is so clear to John it is as though it has already occurred. The crowded little waiting room, Bobbi in the midst of them all, like a star they have come to congratulate. She will be everywhere among them. "Will I come through it?" she will joke. "Hey, I've got wigs I haven't even *worn* yet!" Her speech is not blurred, her eyes are bright as suns. Tall, taller than any of them, she bends to kiss a cheek, to lay a weightless arm on someone's shoulder.

John stands on the edge of this picture, expressionless, as though he is bored. He watches himself curiously, in the way he has noticed that the younger doctors, his own age, sometimes watch him, to see how he is faring. He thinks, observing his own impassive face, how, from the outside, it is impossible to know anything.

He closes his eyes, knowing this is not really the way it will happen. Bobbi will not go to the waiting room: he will lead her, groggy, stumbling, nauseated from the medicine he has already given her tonight, straight to her hospital room, where the others will come to her, one or two at a time, though she will recognize no one. They will bend to kiss her while he stands beside the bed, out of the way. Still, the other scene is truer. It is the one he holds as he falls asleep.

Pepper Hunt

"Did I ever talk to you about pepper?" he asks the girl, who is playing with the plastic pepper shaker, walking it across the table in quick, jerky steps.

She is twelve, a thin girl with fine, limp hair and green-painted fingernails. She has ordered an expensive breakfast, pancakes and eggs with sausage. He hasn't seen her in a few months and dislikes the new assertiveness in her high, childish voice, the way she told the waitress, "I don't want my eggs runny. I won't eat 'em if they're runny."

She does not respond to his question about pepper. She merely gives the shaker a little shove and puts her hands in her lap. Her eyes roam the room incuriously, surfing, he thinks, not really looking at anyone. Their booth is in the nonsmoking section of King's Family Restaurant in the suburb of Pittsburgh, where she lives. It is eight-thirty on a Saturday morning, an in-between time, not that crowded.

"Pepper can be dangerous," he says and waits as the girl's vague pie eyes wander back to his face (that is how he describes her no-color eyes to himself: pie eyes). "When I was your age, my dad and me used to go out in the fields and set out white bread with a lot of pepper on it."

She is gazing at him now with what seems to be full attention, but he is distracted, seeing himself, aged twelve, an undersized boy in overalls, a cowlick of wheat-color hair falling over his forehead. His mother used to sweep back his hair with her hand, to get it out of your eyes, she would say, and there would be the ravaged battleground of his pimpled brow. His mother would freeze for a second before she let the hair fall down again. Over the years his skin has cleared, his body filled out like a tube. His face in middle age is furrowed with fatty deposits. He removes his glasses. He knows he is not a handsome man.

"What'd you do that for?" She tears a strip off her paper napkin and wraps it around a nugget of pink gum she has removed from her mouth. He thinks for a second she's asking why he took off his glasses, then realizes she means the pepper.

"To attract animals," he explains. "Rabbit and deer'd come smelling around the bread. They wouldn't catch on to the pepper at first."

His voice is low and flat, a fact-conveying voice rather than a storytelling voice. And he is conveying facts. He remembers exactly the long, brown fields where he and his father used to go, the clods of bitter-smelling earth that stuck to his heels, the thorny bracken in the ditches at the edge of the fields, not far from this very restaurant where they sit.

"Where would you and your daddy be?" And he knows she means while the rabbits and deer were sniffing around the bread. He likes her question. It shows she's listening and thinking about how it was. Her question is a sign that she is not entirely lost, that she may even have something of him in her.

"We'd be ducked down behind some shrub, him over on one side of the field, me on the other." He no longer sees his father in the picture, only himself in his too-big overalls crouched behind a stand of sumac, clutching his baseball bat.

"Anyways," he continues, anxious to go on with the story, remembering the excitement he felt when the first rabbit appeared, its long ears poking up from the furrows like a cartoon bunny's. Then more ears, as though the rabbits had been hiding there all along. And back in the scrub oak on the edge of the field, the larger, bulkier shadow that is a deer. He (the boy) is laughing soundlessly, his breath coming fast.

"We'd wait there, real quiet, and after a while, the rabbit and deer'd come up and sniff at the pepper bread, and they'd start sneezing. They'd sneeze and sneeze and couldn't stop, jerking all over like they were having some kind of fit. Then we'd run up and beat their brains out."

He stops. The story about pepper is over. The girl is looking at him. Her no-color eyes have not changed. She doesn't say anything. He cannot tell what she's thinking. The waitress sets down their plates. The girl starts to eat immediately. He watches her, feeling as though he has told the story wrong. He wants her to react, to ask another question. But she's pouring syrup over her pancakes and doesn't look at him. He feels uneasy, as though he has left something out.

The waitress returns with coffee and fills his cup. The girl says in her high-pitched, newly assertive voice that she wants coffee, too. The waitress glances at him, pinching her lips. The red of the woman's lipstick has bled into the cracks around her mouth. He nods. She fills the girl's cup and walks away.

He stirs his coffee, sloshing it into the saucer. He is trying to think of another story, but none occurs to him. In his mind, he is still beating the small doe to her knees. Her head is bloodied, but she continues to sneeze convulsively. He leaves off beating her and slams his bat down on a frenzied rabbit. It crumples instantly. He wants the girl to see this, too, but she is cutting her pancakes carefully into small squares.

She says, "Why'n you never take me on a pepper hunt? Your daddy took you. Why'n you never take me?"

He is stunned. She couldn't possibly expect him to take her hunting. Where would they go? The fields where he and his father went with their baseball bats are paved over with housing developments. Though there are other fields, he doesn't know the people who own them.

"Why'd you tell me that story if you weren't gonna take me?" she asks, her mouth full of pancake mush.

"I thought you might want to know something I did when I was a boy." He resents her question. He wants her to ask about the animals so he can describe the pale trickle of brains that oozed from the doe's smashed skull before she stopped breathing, the sneeze that came reflexively after she died. But she does not ask. Her pie eyes regard him malevolently.

"Maybe you're lying to me," she says. "Maybe you never did no pepper hunts. Maybe your daddy just told you about 'em, like you're telling me."

He wonders where the girl gets such thoughts. From her

mother, he guesses, though all he remembers her mother saying when he told her something was "Yeah?", until finally he
couldn't stand it anymore. The girl stares in his direction and
he remembers the doe looking up at him from her knees, the
wet glisten of her frantic eyes as he raises his bat.

"Listen," he says, "I told you that story for a reason. You be
careful what you go sniffing around. That's all I told it for."

And he leans back against the padded seat, relieved to have
found this explanation for telling the story. Still, something
seems awry. He can't think what it is. The girl's plate is empty.
It's time to go. He wonders if she will even remember the story.
She has problems remembering things in school, her mother
has told him.

"Maybe I'll take you hunting," he says.

The girl's no-color eyes focus for an instant. She nods.

"I'll go," she says. "I'll go in a minute."

"Wipe your mouth," he says, easing his body out of the
booth.

Duckie's Okay

୧

She sees him curled in the shallow lee of the door, his little legs tucked under him, his eyes closed, and thinks for a blinding half second he's dead. When she realizes he's sleeping, she's furious.

"Why aren't you inside? Are you locked out? Are you all right?"

Visions of abuse spin through her head. Abuse by the cabby who drives him home from school on days she can't pick him up. Abuse by a spaced-out homeless dopehead who's found his way into her neighborhood. The boy's face as he opens his eyes is so woebegone she feels a thud in her chest. Anger leaks out of her. She kneels and gathers him into her arms. Oh lord, his pants are drenched.

"Junior went home," he murmurs into her shoulder.

"Junior?"

She pictures a hulking pockmarked youth, a ghastly perverted Junior, then remembers the gray cat from up the street.

"I was giving him milk and the door closed."

So, no assault.

"Have you been outside long?"

She won't mention his wetting his pants. They've had a problem with that, though not during the day for a while. Nights are another matter. He's only six.

"A little long," he says.

She kisses him. His hair smells sour. She can't remember when they washed it last.

"We'll go inside and have something good for supper," she promises, trying to remember what they have in the house—Froot Loops, frozen fish sticks, a zillion boxes of that macaroni and cheese he used to like but now won't touch. The heck with it, she thinks. "Listen, Duckie, why don't we order pizza for supper? And I'll go get chocolate milk. Does that sound good?"

The little boy studies her solemnly, his skin pale as paper, his dark eyes opaque. She is always surprised by his noble little face, delicately square with a thin aquiline nose and small rosy lips, mercifully no feature invoking his father except perhaps his eyes—hers are light blue.

As she watches, his eyes take on a familiar crafty glint. "No smelly-smelly?"

"No pepperoni. I promise."

"Just cheese?"

"Double cheese if you want."

He pokes out his lips in satisfaction. Poor little shrimp, she thinks as she helps him up. His legs are streaky with pee.

She reaches for the key in her bag. "Let's go have a bath, and I'll tell you about the people I just showed a house to. They were real Arabs."

"Arabs from the desert?" he wonders, looking up at her.

"Yeah, but they wear clothes like ours." As though she wears Armani suits, Rolex watches, Chanel sheaths. She opens the door and scoops up the mail from the floor, circulars, bills, notices from competing house agents. "I'll run your bath. Then I'll go quick like a rabbit to the market for milk. Okay, Duckie?"

And Gucci shoes, she remembers. The Arabs were wearing Gucci shoes.

Obediently, the little boy follows his mother up the stairs, where he goes into his room, takes off his soiled clothes, and puts them in a pile behind the door. Briefly, he remembers the moment when he knew he couldn't hold it any longer and had to sit down in the doorway and let go. That was after he tricked Junior into their house with a saucer of milk and the cat slurped up the milk; then, when he reached out to hug it, it dashed out the door. He ran out, too, and the door slammed behind him. *Wham! Oh!*

"All set?" his mother asks. "Do you have your toys?"

His toys are lined up along the edge of the tub, a submarine, a broken paddleboat he no longer plays with, and a yellow plastic duck. He carefully lifts a foot over the side of the tub and touches the water with his toe. His mother sometimes forgets to check the temperature. He eases down into the tub. The water comes to the middle of his chest. He lifts a foot out to see if his skin is turning that funny shade of pink. Oh, it is!

He begins moving the submarine around on top of the water. The sub is looking for the duck floating on the other side of his knee. "Absolute idiot!" he hears his mother exclaim. She is in her room talking out loud the way she sometimes does. He asked her once who she talked to, and she said, "To myself, Duckie. I tell myself all those smart things I wish I'd said to somebody else." Usually he catches only phrases, like "Tell me another one!" or "Who do you think you are—Superman?" She has never spoken to him in that way, only to the person she addresses when she talks to herself. He feels sorry for that person—his father maybe, though his father lives somewhere else, now, and his mother no longer mentions him as much as she used to. The Prince of Darkness, she likes to call his father. *The Prince of Darkness was late with the check again,* she'll say on the phone. Or, *No, we haven't heard from the Prince for a while.* The boy paddles his legs up and down, making waves so that the duck floats around behind him out of the reach of the submarine. "Why, thank you. I'd love to," his mother says in an entirely different tone.

He lets the submarine go and turns over on his stomach. He lowers his face into the water, then draws it out quickly, gasping. He dunks his face under the water one more time, then sits up. The duck is bobbing in front of him. He steers the submarine toward it.

"Are you using soap?" His mother comes into the bathroom wearing jeans and a yellow T-shirt. Her hair is loose and fuzzy, the way he likes it, not the way she wears it to work, pulled back tight in the shape of a football. She looks soft and pretty now. He has an urge to hold out his arms to her, but he knows she won't hug him when he's wet.

"We really need to wash your hair," she says, frowning.

His hair! He opens his mouth to wail. He rarely makes loud

sounds, and when he does, they frighten him. They frighten his mother, too.

"We'll do it tomorrow," she says quickly and leans down and kisses the top of his head. "Will you be okay if I go get the chocolate milk now?"

He nods his head yes. He is watching the wily duck trying to slip around his knee to escape the sub.

"You won't drown or anything?"

No. He shakes his head. The submarine is closing in. His mother is going downstairs. He paddles a little with his legs to make the duck move away as the submarine comes closer. He wonders why his mother is in a good mood. They have not had pizza or chocolate milk since his grandmother came to visit and they had treats every day. His grandmother loves treats. It's too bad pizza isn't his favorite food as his mother believes, but he doesn't want her face to go saggy as it did when he told her he hated, *hated* macaroni and cheese. The chocolate milk will be good. He will try to trick Junior with the milk if there's any left tomorrow. He hears the front door click. The house is suddenly empty in a way that scares and excites him. She will be back soon, he reminds himself as he always does. She is only going to the store on the corner.

She walks quickly past the brick town houses with their small, mostly well-kept gardens. Houses sell well in this neighborhood, or they did before the bottom dropped out of the real estate market last year. It is an older downtown neighborhood, *très* desirable, where a renovated carriage house has been known to go for five hundred grand, and where she can't really afford to live since the divorce. She had a good run of sales before the market collapsed; lately she's had to dip into her savings to pay her rent. But she can't imagine living anywhere else. Her little boy took his first steps in the park up the street and later rode his Big Wheel up and down the graveled paths while she and her girlfriends sat around a picnic table talking and laughing themselves silly. Those were great years, when she and her friends, smart, good-looking, in-your-face women, got together with their kids in the park. Nearly all of them have money troubles, now, men troubles, you name it. She isn't the only one.

She tries to speed up her pace, but her clogs slow her down. Of course, she shouldn't have left the boy alone in the bathtub. She's done it before; still, if anybody found out, they might haul her into court. The District of Columbia is known to come down hard on single mothers. The boy could be sent to live in Manhattan with the Prince, who is so hot on his great journalistic career he doesn't have time to go to the bathroom. But nobody will find out and nothing will happen to her precious little duck. She forces herself to walk faster. She feels her chest tightening, that nervous crazy feeling coming back. What is wrong with her? A second ago she was thinking about the park where she and her little boy have had so many good times. *King high!* he used to scream as she pushed him on the baby swing. *King high!*

She is out of breath when she arrives at the corner. It's the smoking. One day she will quit, after she has her life under control. The light turns green and she crosses. She wonders whether Ng is working at the market today or whether it's the unpleasant woman who owns the store. She draws a breath and coughs, hoping it is Ng.

The little boy sits still, holding the submarine trapped under his thigh. The duck comes floating innocently from around his back. He waits, not moving, until the duck drifts far enough forward that it can't easily float back to safety, then he lets the submarine pop up. It hits the duck directly from below. "Got him!" he whispers and grabs the duck and tosses it over the side of the tub onto the floor, where it lands with a *plop, plop,* and lies still. He closes his eyes and smiles. His mother thinks he doesn't like his duck because of the way he treats it, but he does like it, he *does.*

He takes the soap and begins moving it over his skin, over his legs and tummy and shoulders. As he moves the soap around, it keeps spurting out of his hands and sinking to the bottom of the tub and he has to feel around to find it. After a while, he gets tired of searching and decides the soap should stay down there and drown.

The air feels cool on his skin. He slides down so that the water covers his shoulders. Then he turns over and pretends to swim, moving his legs and arms the way he saw people doing at the pool his mother took him to last summer. Water sloshes out onto the floor. He raises his head and looks over the side of the tub. There's a lot of water on the floor; the green tiles shimmer like the surface of a swimming pool. In the middle of the pool, the duck lies on its side.

He listens to see if his mother has returned but hears only

the hollow breathing of the empty house. He sees a shadow on the bottom of the tub: the soap, now slim as a finger. He grabs at it but it gets away. He puts his face under water again. The water covers his ears and blanks out the emptiness of the house, filling his head with the sound of gentle drumming. The sensation is peaceful, not scary at all.

"Those Arabs spent two hours looking at the house," she tells Ng. "We're up and down the stairs, checking out the pool, the garage. I'm blabbing about the insulation, the new pipes, the copper wiring, then the guy goes, 'Infrastructure is not a concern, madam.'"

Ng nods. He is wearing a University of Atlantic City sweatshirt, trying to look American, she guesses. Is there a university in Atlantic City?

"They obviously have more money than God," she goes on, and tells him about the big Lincoln parked in the no-parking zone and how the Arabs talked to each other in low voices, speaking English with a snooty Brit accent, acting as though she was just there to open doors.

"You think they buy the house?" Ng asks.

"They said they'd get back to me. We're talking 10.3 mil asking price."

"Big bucks." Ng eyes the quart of chocolate milk, Camel Lites, and roll of mints she has put on the counter. "That all you getting?"

"I need this sale, Ng."

"Hey, you're a big shot, Mrs. Kemper. I see your name on For Sale signs all over the neighborhood. Picture, too."

"Nobody's selling right now. Top agents are spending their Sundays showing condos to twenty-five-year-olds."

"Maybe it's your turn for luck. You sure you don't want anything else?"

"No-o-o. Just put these items on my bill."

"Sorry. Can't do that, Mrs. Kemper. Boss says no more credit."

"Come on, Ng." Hasn't she always paid in the end?

Ng shrugs and looks out the window.

"Okay, okay." She reaches in her bag and pulls out the five-dollar bill left from lunch and puts it on the counter. "I've got to hurry. I left my son in the tub."

God, she thinks, why did I say that?

But Ng acts as though he didn't hear. He's toting up her bill. "Cigarettes three-sixty, milk one-thirty, mints eighty-five. With tax it comes to five-ninety."

"I can't believe it! I'm going to have to put it on my card."

Ng shrugs again. She fumbles in her bag. There's the zippered pocket where she keeps emergency cab fare, but she won't touch that. She feels a heaviness in her chest.

"Too bad you're low on cash," Ng says. "I got some good shit today."

For a moment they are silent. She glances around. The only other customer is a middle-aged woman in a blue pants suit bending over the cheese compartment.

"You got an extra twenty?" Ng asks. "We forget about the extra on the groceries."

She's been clean for two weeks. The heaviness in her chest seems to expand into her arms and legs, weighing her down, while her brain is zinging out into crazy zone. It's the fear, always the fear that something will happen to her little boy. Finding him on the doorstep like he was dead! That's what has put her over the top.

"Excuse me." It is the other customer, brandishing a wedge of Brie. "Do you mind—?"

"Go ahead," she says and moves off down an aisle, her clogs thumping the wood floor.

Excuse me. Do you mind—The woman reminds her of her mother, apologizing but butting in just the same. The woman even has those brown beauty-parlor curls like her mother, and her clothes might have come from the Junior League Shop. *Oh, I got the cutest Calvin Klein today. Cuffed pants and just my shade of blue. Only twenty dollars—*

She hears the woman chitchatting to Ng, hears the register chime, hears the woman say, "Thank you *so very* much," and then the door bangs.

She returns to the counter.

"Da-da-a-a!"

She dangles a bill in front of Ng, the twenty from the zippered pocket. A new twenty that looks like Monopoly money.

"Well?" she says.

Ng reaches under the counter.

"I'm in a hurry, Ng." She's still short on the groceries and she doesn't want to owe the Chink. She reaches out and flicks the roll of mints with her finger. It shoots off the other side of the counter onto the floor.

"Oops. Sorry." *Excuse me.*

Ng ignores the mints. He puts the milk and cigarettes and a plastic envelope into a paper bag.

"How's your kid anyhow?" he says.

She doesn't answer. Her son isn't his fucking business. She picks up the grocery bag.

"'Bye, Mrs. Kemper," Ng says, but she doesn't answer. She walks out of the store holding her bag against her chest.

"I'm back," she calls in a croaky breathless voice. "Duckie?" Silence.

"Answer me, Duckie. I have the milk. Are you okay?"

She fumbles with the bag, shaking powder onto one of the circulars that came in the mail, breathing it up, breathing it in, taking a deep deep—

The little boy still doesn't answer. She drops the paper on the table. "Duckie!" She begins pounding up the stairs. It takes her forever to get to the top, as though she were on a treadmill. As she labors up, she promises herself never never never—Please God, never never never. Please. God. Never. Never—

He looks at her with eyes that seem both sad and loving. Such a noble little face. Her heart beats frantically as though it will leap out of her chest. She'd been clean for two weeks. She and the Prince used to zone out on weekends, then forget about it. Since he left—

Silently, she picks the little boy up out of the water and wraps him in a towel, then kneels on the sopping floor, holding him against her. His skin is shriveled like a newborn's. She loves him so damn much. Oh why was he ever born? Her heart thuds, thuds.

"Duckie," she says. "I'm so sorry."

"Don't call me that," he murmurs in a thin, stuffy voice.

"What?"

"I said don't call me that."

"Duckie? I always call you Duckie. Aw, you're just mad at me for taking so long at the store. *Duckie.*"

She feels lighter now, lifting off. Man, it's good.

"Don't!" he whimpers.

She laughs, she can't help it. He's so funny when he's mad. "Duckie," she says.

He wrenches himself out of her arms and slides down onto the cold, wet floor. The duck bobs up beside him, grinning. His yellow duck, alive and well. He wants to reach out his arms.

His mother is looking at him, her eyes huge. He glares back at her. She shouldn't tease him. Teasing is bad.

She gets to her feet. "Damn. I'm soaked. Where are your pajamas?"

She shoves her fingers through her hair and goes out.

The little boy shivers. He looks at the duck with its grinning beak. He reaches out and flattens the yellow face with his hand, then lets go. *Pop!* It's back. The boy smiles. "No I *won't* excuse you," he hears his mother say in the next room. He scrunches the duck's face again, then drops it on the floor. "I will *never* forgive you." His foot shoots out and, *wham!*, the duck flies across the wet floor and hits the wall. *Plam!* "You have ruined my life—" It lies there on its side, motionless, but he knows that the duck really really really is okay.

You Won't Remember This

❧

Angelina lay in a green canvas chair in her garden and watched a white butterfly play among her flowers. She had never in her life sat still long enough to watch a butterfly; even as a child, she was always busy. "High-strung," her mother used to tell her, "you were a high-strung child." "It's so good to see you sit," her mother said now, as though her sitting meant that Angelina was content. In fact, she felt like a creature that had been washed up on a strange and beautiful shore. Her body was swollen from all the liquid it retained in the summer heat. She had no energy even to think. The baby seemed torpid as well; it no longer struggled inside her, but occasionally gave a languid kick as though to remind her it was still there, in no hurry to come out.

At first, when she found out she was pregnant, she had reacted in the same brisk, efficient manner she was known for in her professional life. She chose an obstetrician, a well-known, respected doctor, and assembled a wardrobe of maternity clothes, many of them borrowed from friends since she did not expect to wear them again. She read books on the first nine months of life, studying pictures of the fetus at each stage in its growth, trying to relate them to the changes in her own slim body, to the thickening and swelling and soreness, to the ugly spots that appeared on her face, to the shift in her sense of balance that caused her to be always conscious of the way she walked and stood and sat.

At night, before she and her husband went to bed, they practiced the exercises for childbirth they learned in a special class. They were both determined to do everything right, her husband especially. "No, you're not relaxed enough," he would say, holding up her leg under the knee and letting it drop. "You need to relax more. Take a deep breath." Then, while she practiced the little panting breaths she had been taught, he would hold his face close over hers, panting, too, his eyes fixed, his mouth opening and closing like a fish's.

She went to work every morning as usual, coming home a little more tired each day. "Why don't you take off these last few weeks?" her husband suggested. "You don't want to be too tired when the baby comes." But she kept going to the office until the doctor told her the swelling was too great; she would have to stay at home where she could keep her legs up. "It won't be long now," he said.

By then, her mother had come to help her finish getting ready. "You just sit. I will do everything," her mother said, making Angelina remember how it had been when she was a child and her mother did everything. She did not argue, but sat while her mother cooked their meals and prepared the room where the baby would sleep. "I feel guilty letting you do all this work," she said, watching her mother weed the garden in the heat of the day. "Don't be silly," her mother replied. "That's what I'm here for." And Angelina did not protest anymore, but lay quietly inside her great body, watching the white butterfly flit around her garden, never stopping anywhere very long, only an instant, before flitting on again.

Her mother went out and bought everything the baby would need and came back and showed Angelina the little white T-shirts and flowered kimonos with strings that tied at the bottom and a few exquisite tiny gowns with tucks and embroidered rosebuds. "They'll be used only once, you know," she told her mother, and then regretted saying this because it seemed she was ungrateful.

"Oh, and look at this," her mother said, holding up a length of yellow satin ribbon. "It's for the bassinet." The white wicker bassinet that had been Angelina's when she was a baby. Her mother had given it away but found it again, in someone's attic, and brought it to her. "I thought you might like to have this," her mother had said. "I remember so well when you were a baby in this bassinet."

While her mother was out shopping, she rested in the white bedroom she shared with her husband. Everything in this room was white; the walls and ceiling were painted white, the shutters that enclosed the windows were white, even the bedspread was white. One afternoon, while she was resting, a fly got trapped in the room. It hurled itself frenziedly against the window panes, trying to get out, then careened around the room, ricocheting off walls and ceiling. The black fly seemed particularly horrible in all the white. But she did not have the energy to get up and let it out, or kill it. When her mother returned, Angelina in was in tears, lying on the white bed. "Why, what's wrong? Is it the baby?" her mother asked. Angelina did not answer, only lay there, tears streaming down her face. Her mother stroked her forehead. "Can I get you anything?" She did not seem to notice the fly. "I'll bring you a glass of iced tea." On her way out of the room, her mother picked up a magazine and killed the fly, neatly, with one stroke, on the windowsill. Angelina fell asleep in the silence that followed the death of the fly.

When she could not stand sitting anymore, she took her heavy body out for a walk, moving slowly in the wet heat, her mind unusually alert. She noticed everything, all the elaborate details of the downtown neighborhood where she and her husband lived—the window boxes planted with fern and geranium, the filigreed porch lamps, the iron fences, the carved stone lions on either side of a door, the subtle colors of the houses, mauve, salmon, fawn, honey.

During these walks, she felt curiously at a distance from everything, the way a traveler might feel traveling alone in a strange country. The feeling was not unpleasant. Inside her swollen body, she knew she was free to go anywhere, to look at anything, without fear or self-consciousness, the way she imagined a man must always feel. She no longer avoided the glances of strangers on the street or closed her ears to their remarks. When men with dancing eyes grinned at her as they passed, she smiled radiantly back at them. She knew they were not looking at her.

One day, passing a restaurant a few blocks from her house, she glanced in the window and saw a man she knew sitting at the bar. He was a heavy, dark, sensual man, older than she was; she had had a short affair with him before she married her husband. She stood at the window watching the man, thinking maliciously that if he looked up and saw her now, he would be ashamed and embarrassed. While she watched, standing close to the glass, the man stood up and she saw that he was with a woman, a thin, pretty, red-haired woman, who was laughing at something the man had said. They laughed together so heartily that Angelina began to laugh, too. She was still laughing when they passed her, on their way out of the restaurant, almost touching her. The man did not even glance at her, and she knew that she was right: she had become invisible. She walked slowly home, dragging her body through the oppressive heat, stopping often to rest because the baby's weight now pressed like boulders on her legs.

At home, her mother had changed into a pearl-gray dress and darkened her lashes. She thought how young and attractive her mother looked. In the middle of the table, her mother had placed a cut-glass bowl filled with deep pink roses from the garden and beside the bowl, a pair of heavy silver candelabra. "How beautiful everything is," Angelina said.

Her mother looked at her anxiously. "You've been gone a long time. Shouldn't you rest? Can I get you anything?"

"I'm going to sit outside," she said and went out into the garden and sank her enormous body into the green canvas chair, the only chair in which she could now be comfortable. Even here, she felt restless, as though all of her nerves were on edge, and she wanted to scream. Nevertheless, by the time her mother came out with a glass of cold tea for her, she lay still, her eyes closed.

When she woke, she heard her mother and her husband talking in the kitchen. Their voices were low and intense. "Maybe she'll decide not to go back to work at all," her mother was saying. Her husband said, "Oh, she's too good at what she does. She'd be bored at home. We'll get a nanny for the baby." "Yes, but she ought to take some time off," her mother insisted. "She's always tried to do too much. I worry about her." "Don't worry," her husband said. "She'll be fine. I promise you."

She listened in a detached way. It was as though they were discussing someone she did not know. Then she became irritated listening to the argument. She struggled to get out of her chair, but fell back heavily each time she tried. She began to laugh at her clumsiness; her laughter grew loud and shrill, until it was almost hysterical. Her husband and her mother came running out into the garden. "Are you all right?" her mother asked. Her husband bent over her, his eyes large and anxious, his face close to hers. "I'm fine," she sobbed, trying to control herself because of the pain that had started in her side. "When are we going to eat? I'm starving," though she had not thought of food until that moment. Her mother said, "I'll put it on right away," and hurried back into the house. Her husband begged, "Tell me how you feel." He put his hand on her stomach where the baby was moving continuously, causing tiny ripples like waves just under the skin. Immediately, he took his hand away, and she thought, *It won't be long now.*

At dinner she ate ravenously, tearing off chunks of bread and putting them into her mouth with pieces of tender veal.

Her husband and her mother looked at her thoughtfully. "She certainly seems to be eating for two tonight," her mother said. "Yes," her husband agreed, "everything she does affects the baby." He paused and her mother said, "You've prepared yourselves so carefully. You've thought of everything, including the birth itself. You even know how to breathe!" Her mother laughed. "These things used to be handed down from mother to daughter. But I was knocked out the whole time. I wouldn't know what to say."

Angelina was so full that her stomach pressed painfully against her ribs, pushing up under her lungs so she could hardly breathe. She sat very still thinking if she did not move, she could not suffocate, but the pressure increased until she felt her stomach might rise into her throat. She tried to breathe using the little panting breaths she had been taught in the class, but they did not help. She felt dizzy and gripped the armrests of her chair to keep from falling over. "Here's to a wonderful dinner," she heard her husband say. He looked flushed and handsome in the candlelight, and she could tell from his voice that he was a little drunk. "And here's to many more good dinners," her mother responded gaily. She held up her glass. Angelina's husband held up his, too, and after a moment, Angelina picked up her glass of tea. She had a brilliant smile on her face, despite the fact that she was suffocating. They reached toward each other, but the table was too large for the glasses to touch.

"Don't you want some coffee?" her mother asked. "No, thank you," Angelina said, getting up from her place. "Please excuse me." She went into the garden, carrying her enormous body slowly and carefully, breathing in small shallow breaths through her mouth. Outside it was dark; all around her were the bright unwinking lights of houses and apartment buildings and above, the glow of the city had turned the sky a vivid pink, as though there were a fire somewhere. A siren wailed, making her think of the way a wolf's howl must sound in the wilderness. I am not used to this, she thought. I have never known any of this before.

She paced slowly over the swept brick, panting as the pain rose, breathing deeply when it receded. You will not feel pain, they had told her in the class, only pressure, as the baby tries to get out, and you will handle it by breathing and by concentrating on something. Now she realized they had deceived her, the way people sometimes deceive children by telling them it won't hurt or it will only hurt for a minute.

When her husband and her mother came out onto the porch, she was walking slowly around the small garden, staring fixedly at the ground. Her husband came up to her and said, "It's the baby, isn't it?" When she did not reply, he said, "Don't you want to come inside and lie down?" He reached out to touch her but she drew back with such a fierce mute stare that he went quickly back up on the porch.

"Why does she have that look on her face?" asked her mother in bewilderment. "She's concentrating, that's all," said her husband. "There's nothing to worry about. After all, women used to drop their babies in the middle of a field and go right on working." Her mother turned to him with a shocked look and he said quickly, "I'm sorry. I don't know why I said that."

After a few minutes, her husband went out to her again. "We ought to call the doctor now, darling." Angelina gave him another terrible look and went on with her pacing and he went inside and called. "I'm afraid she's beginning to panic," he told the doctor. "She won't speak to me." But the doctor reassured him. "That's natural. She's concentrating. Just find out how far apart the contractions are and call me back."

Her husband made himself a large drink and took it into the living room, where her mother sat holding a magazine. "I can't watch her anymore," her mother said. "There's nothing I can do to help her." She began to weep soundlessly. "Please don't cry," her husband said. "Everything is fine. Maybe you could go and see whether her bag is ready." "Yes, I'll do that," her mother said, wiping her eyes. She glanced at the stopwatch he was holding. "What on earth is that for?" "It's to time the contractions," her husband explained. Her mother shook her head sorrowfully. "I'm sorry I can't help you," she said as she started upstairs. "I was knocked out the whole time. I really don't know anything about it."

Angelina continued walking, taking deep sighing breaths and holding her belly until another pain came and then she breathed in quick gasps and let her arms fall to her sides because she could not stand to touch herself. Her husband walked beside her with his stopwatch, trying to guess when the contractions came from the changes in her breathing. After a while, he said, "Eleven minutes. They're eleven minutes apart," and went back inside to call the doctor. When he left, she looked up quickly at the glowing red sky that seemed to have grown brighter, more livid, since she began to pace. Then her womb contracted and she lowered her head and clenched her fists. It took all her determination to keep moving. Her husband stood on the porch and watched her plodding around the garden holding her enormous stomach, her legs like an elephant's, her head bent onto her breast. Just like an animal, he thought, and quickly stopped himself and thought instead about the baby, his child, that was about to be born.

Though she did not want to leave the garden, she was finally too tired to walk and she let her husband help her into the car. She lay on her side in the backseat, no longer trying to keep track of the pains as she had been taught, of the way each one approached, swept over her, and receded. She heard her husband talking to himself. "We're into the second stage now. Contractions five minutes apart. Doing fine." She kept her eyes open and stared at the fantastic designs of light that played on the car seat when they passed a neon sign or street lamp. "How's it going back there?" her husband asked. But she said nothing. She remained mute even after they reached the hospital, never speaking when they strapped her onto the table under the brash lights, or when the nurses touched her with their cool needle-like hands, or when the doctor gave instructions in his calm objective voice. At last, when volcanic eruptions seized her just before the baby was born, she broke her silence and uttered terrific neighing grunts of pleasure.

After that, she lay quietly, her eyes shut. When she opened them, her husband was bending over her, his face close to hers, his large dark eyes glowing with tears. She looked at him, wondering what she wanted to say to him.

"Hello," she said finally.

"We have a baby," he replied, as though in answer to a question.

"Yes," she said.

"You were wonderful," he said.

"No," she objected. "I wasn't."

"It's over now. Everything's fine."

Angelina felt terribly angry about something. She looked around the room for the first time; everything was white: white walls and ceilings, white lights, doctor and nurses in white, her husband white except for his dark eyes above the white mask. She too was covered with white as she lay on the table.

"Don't you want to see her?" her husband asked. "She's beautiful. She looks just like you."

Angelina lifted her head and stared at her stomach, which was now flat and lifeless, on which the baby lay. All she could see was the baby's head, shiny and pointed, covered with long black hair.

"Like me? Don't be silly," she said and lay back again.

A nurse picked up the baby and put it in the bend of Angelina's arm. Angelina studied its angry red face and swollen slits of eyes through which the baby seemed to regard her hostilely. Suddenly, like a small furious animal, it burrowed its face into her side. She pushed it away, horrified.

"You plan to nurse your baby, don't you?" the nurse said.

"Of course she does," her husband replied. "We've read all about it. We know it's the best way."

She lay completely passive while they pulled the sheet down from her breast and turned her so the baby could reach the nipple. At first, the baby could not find what it wanted; it gnawed at the side of her breast and the skin under her arm, until the nurse took the nipple in her fingers and shoved it into the baby's mouth. Angelina cried out at the sharp pain when the baby clamped onto her tender flesh. Then she sobbed in great noisy gasps while the baby pulled and sucked, stabbing her repeatedly with pain.

Her husband tried to wipe away her tears with his sleeve. "Darling, sweetheart, don't." He looked distraught. He rushed off and came back with tissues with which he dabbed at her face. After a while, the baby fell asleep, exhausted, and the nurse picked it up. "We'll bring her to you in your room in about an hour," the nurse told her. "Please don't," Angelina said. "I want to sleep."

The nurse glanced at her and went out carrying the baby. "You'll feel better after you rest," her husband said. "I'm going to call your mother now." He kissed her and hurried away.

They took her back to her room, a small soft-beige room with gentle lighting. She got into bed and yawned luxuriously. Her body felt light and free. She happened to notice her foot and saw how thin it was again, how white and delicate with its tracing of blue veins. For a moment, she felt full of impatience, ready to leap up and run out to do all the things she used to take pleasure in doing. But in reality, she was so tired she could not even lift her hand. Now she would sleep and when she woke, her child would be there and she would nurse it and do everything for it. Angelina made a little mewing sound in her throat. It was all so irresistible, yet it had nothing to do with her. She lay listening to the rushing traffic on the street below her window, which sounded like waves beating on a shore, and thought of a white beach, an inlet curled like a woman's fingernail, and a jutting of bleached rock on which a still dark figure lay.

Then the nurse came in with the baby. Angelina felt a stirring in her breasts. Gingerly, she put her lips to the baby's forehead. The baby's warmth shocked her and she drew back, but she couldn't resist and kissed the baby again. What was it she had been thinking about? She couldn't remember. How strange. Someone had warned her: You won't remember, afterward. She had thought they were talking about the pain.

George, Nadia, Blaise

&

It is one of those warm October days meant for long walks or picnics, especially here in this beautiful spot overlooking the Shenandoah Valley. On any other day like this, George and Nadia, who own the small clapboard farmhouse on this mountainside, would be outside with their four children enjoying the sun and clean air, which is what they drive out here for, nearly every weekend, from Washington. Instead, they are inside, dusting, scrubbing, doing all the household chores they come to the farm to escape. At any moment, a friend whom they have not seen in fifteen years will arrive: hence, the compulsive cleanup, though they both know that Blaise Dupres will not notice—or care—whether the house is free of cobwebs or not. Blaise's eyes will be focused on entirely different things.

"Do you think he's mellowed?" George asks, wiping dust from the windowsill.

Nadia is kneeling on the hearth of the huge granite fireplace, arranging logs for the fire they will have that evening.

"I doubt it," she replies. "I expect he's the same old Blaise."

It has been so long since they have seen him George wonders what Nadia means by *same old Blaise*. George's image is of a thickly built man with flowing white hair riding a Harley-Davidson with a woman, a very young woman, on the back.

"You're probably right," he says and wipes the mullions.

Nadia heaves on another log. Small and fragile-looking, she is actually quite strong, stronger than George, whose back gives him trouble. Though he is only forty-five, he can no longer pick up their youngest, four-year-old Carla, without pain.

Now he giggles. "Remember how the man could talk?"

Nadia makes a low noise, like a snort. He has heard this snort before. When did she begin to make that funny strangled sound?

"What is this, George? A nostalgia trip?"

"The man was once my idol," George reminds her. "I went through my entire antiwar experience with him. I became an environmentalist because of him. We filed *law*suits together, for Christ's sake."

He grins. He is not serious, or not entirely serious, but how should he express the importance of Blaise Dupres in his life? It is not enough to say that Blaise was once his law professor at the school where George himself now teaches, before Blaise left Washington for Berkeley, where for a time he was a spokesman—an important one—for peace groups and environmentalists. Blaise is still occasionally quoted in news stories on these issues. George always saves the articles for Nadia to read, though these issues have nothing to do with why Blaise is important to either of them.

"Of course," he adds, "I never rode a motorcycle behind him."

Their eyes meet. Nadia flushes, the way she used to do when George first met her at a peace vigil in front of the White House, when she was nineteen.

"Damn you," she says, mouthing the words so the children, upstairs, will not hear. Then she grins, letting him know she is not serious either, not entirely.

On the slope below the house are several dozen apple trees, heavy with small bronze fruit the size of a child's fist. The apple trees remind George of a picnic they had—he, Nadia, Blaise—fifteen years ago. It is an occasion he and Nadia have often discussed. At the time, George had known her for exactly one month and was desperately in love.

"You were snozzled" is what she always says when they talk about the picnic.

Now, peering through the window at the orchard, he remembers Nadia sitting cross-legged on a blanket, her long dark hair framing her small face. When she raised her hand to shield her eyes from the sun, her delicate wrist reminded him—still reminds him—of the fine bones of those African antelopes in the Washington zoo.

Blaise was stretched out beside her, a big man with strong blunt features, very blue eyes, prematurely white hair. George recalls him gesturing grandly over the valley, talking about something—apples, justice, the lawsuit he and George were planning to bring to prevent the government from building a dam farther down the valley. Who knows what Blaise was talking about?

Nadia always says, "He kept giving me *wine.* I thought, here is this brilliant man and I'm so sleepy I can't follow a word he's saying."

And off to one side, George envisions himself, thin, bespectacled, his soft brown hair tied back in a ponytail, gazing at them both, adoringly.

"All you talked about, George, was cows. You were going to move out here to the family farm, right? Install cows, right?" In their discussions, she imitates his cocky, high-pitched voice. " 'Cows are *easy,* man. They just stay down in the pasture and eat.' You didn't know a damn thing about cows," she usually adds, and of course she is right.

He glances over at his wife kneeling on the hearth. Her waist has thickened over the years and her breasts seem larger. She tends to wear clothes that hide her breasts, such as the loose jeans jumper she has on now. Her hair is still black, but now it is short, shorter, in fact, than George's wavy, light-brown hair, which he still wears long, though not in a ponytail. It occurs to George that he would like to tell Nadia how pretty she looks right now, but he doubts this is the right time, when she is wrestling with that large hickory log.

Just then, loud shrieks come from overhead. Thuds, thumps, louder screams.

"What's going on up there?" Nadia calls, her voice calm but also threatening.

A babble of loud cries answers her, to George indecipherable and awful.

"Damn," Nadia mutters. She drops the log, lurches to her feet, and charges up the stairs, her Dr. Scholl's clattering like castanets.

"Mike! Laurel!" Her commanding voice reaches George clearly through the drafty interstices of the old house, filling him with admiration. The fragile girl he married is a fearsomely competent mother.

"I want you to pick up these cards, pronto," he hears her say, not angrily, but with great firmness. "Justin, let go of your little sister. Clean this mess up, guys. We're expecting company."

George sighs and dust flies up and clouds his glasses. He takes them off, pulls out a handkerchief and wipes them, thinking of another voice, deep, sonorous, also full of authority: "It's time we got together again, George. I'm here with Hugo for a few days. Just got in from Managua. How about it?"

Managua? Impulsively, George invited Blaise and his son Hugo to drive out to the farm on Sunday—today—for dinner with him and Nadia and the children. All Nadia said when he told her was, "Blaise Dupres? You're kidding!" Then she flushed in the old way.

For something else happened fifteen years ago with Blaise Dupres. Nadia called it an *affair,* George a *seduction.* Whatever it was, not long after the picnic George remembers so vividly, Nadia went off with Blaise on his Harley for a week of drugs and sex, a betrayal (by Blaise; Nadia was too young to know better) that George has long since gotten over, though at the time, he wanted never to see or speak to Blaise again—and in fact, they have not spoken until the phone call the other day. But Blaise has remained a ghostly figure in their marriage. Whenever his name comes up, they invariably look at each other, Nadia with a flush on her small dark face, George with love and pride that she came back, after all, to him.

"Friends!"

Blaise fills the doorway, holding his arms out wide. His massive face, now bearded, is still handsome, the cheeks deeply furrowed, skin tanned, eyes amazingly blue. Blaise is much less of a wreck than George has expected. He looks in some ways better—thinner, less bloated—than he looked fifteen years ago. His white hair is cut modishly short and in his jeans, jeans jacket, and boots, he could be at least ten years younger than his real age, sixty.

"Friends!" he bellows, again.

He is holding aloft a paper donkey on a stick. Covered with bright blue curls of confetti, the donkey is the size of a large dog. He waves it in front of George, Nadia, and the assembled children.

"A gift from my friends, the people of Nicaragua!" he booms, looks piercingly at the children, and growls, "Full of candy."

There is a stunned silence until Nadia exclaims, "A piñata! Great!" and rushes forward to embrace Blaise and intercept the donkey. The children twitter and hold up their hands for their present.

"Hey, welcome, man," George says, a little stiffly. Possibly Blaise does not hear him in the clamor of the children, who are leaping around and demanding candy. Mercifully, they are diverted by Hugo, a big man like his father, black-bearded, gentle, a favorite of theirs. When Blaise went out to California, Hugo, then twelve, and his mother, Blaise's wife Nora, stayed behind, permanently as it turned out. Now Nora lives in Pennsylvania. Hugo, in his late twenties, lives not far from this farm, in Winchester, where he works as a carpenter.

Carla shrieks as Hugo throws her up into the air. The boys tackle him, while Laurel, too old at eleven to join in this hullabaloo, hovers in the background.

"Monkey," laughs Hugo, throwing Carla up again. Then he winks at Laurel, who, overjoyed that he has noticed her, blushes, like her mother.

Meanwhile, Nadia bears the donkey away. For now, she tells the children, she will put it on the mantel among the vases of wildflowers, where it will be safe and happy. The donkey will *like* being with all those flowers.

"Who wants to pick some apples?" Hugo is asking.

It occurs to George that *he* would like to take his children apple-picking, but of course he will not. He and Nadia will entertain Blaise here in the house. Blaise is not the kind of person who is interested in children or apple-picking. In fact, Blaise still stands in the doorway as though contemplating retreat from this child-infested house. George steps forward and holds out his hand.

"Hey, man." He tries again. "Welcome."

For a moment, Blaise stares at him as though he is thinking, Who *are* these people? Then he gives a kind of roar, opens his arms and enfolds George in a strong, loving hug. George hears himself giggling, a violent nervous sound over Blaise's deep subterranean chuckle. George is terrified.

Rich odors of greens and baking apples waft through the door into the living room, where George, Nadia, and Blaise sit talking. George sniffs contentedly. His absurd reaction to Blaise has vanished. He feels happy and proud. It will be a good dinner; Nadia is an excellent cook. Right now, they are listening to Blaise tell about his travels in Nicaragua, from which he has just returned, again. He's gone there often over the years, meeting with poets, writers, old Sandinistas.

"I can tell you, Nadia, it's still bad down there. People have no idea," Blaise says.

This is in response to something Nadia has asked him. She is sitting on the floor threading goldenrod into bracelets. Blaise looks at her meditatively.

Now Blaise launches into a story about something that happened to him on one of his trips, years ago, during the war.

"I drove out into the country, near the mountains." He is still gazing at Nadia. "A woman was walking along the road carrying something in a large handkerchief. The driver stopped to ask her whether she'd seen any fighting. In answer, she showed us what she was carrying. It was a head, severed at the neck. She said it was her son's head, all she'd found of him. My colleague asked who killed him. The woman just stared at him. Then she said, 'His brothers.'"

George and Nadia say nothing in response to this terrible

story, though Nadia has stopped threading the goldenrod; her hands lie still in her lap.

Now Blaise shifts his attention to George.

"Ah, George! Let me tell you about a friend of mine, a man I guarantee you would like. The former minister of culture under the Sandinistas, a graduate of Columbia, a poet, a brilliant man. My host on this last trip."

Blaise tells them how he and this man stayed up whole nights talking about revolution and poetry. Can George and Nadia guess the officer's favorite American poet?

"Walt Whitman," guesses George without thinking.

"Ginsberg," says Nadia.

"Emily Dickinson," Blaise says. "Isn't that remarkable?"

Through the window, George sees his children racing across the field, followed by Hugo, who lopes along with surprising grace for such a big man, Carla riding his shoulders. Now the three oldest children begin climbing a sugar maple whose leaves have turned a blinding red. He loves seeing them out in the field like that, having such a good time.

Nadia says, "I guess I ought to do something about dinner."

But she does not get up. Wreathed in goldenrod, she looks radiant. She could be nineteen.

"Little mother," Blaise says, in his gravelly sexy voice, "you are beautiful."

For a moment, there is silence. George feels proud, then embarrassed. How can Blaise say such things after all that's happened?

Nadia ducks her head. "Aw, I'm gettin' fat."

Blaise chuckles lasciviously. His blue eyes are clear, his teeth unbelievably white. Didn't they hear he was once hospitalized for something fairly serious? Drugs maybe? An overdose? How can he look so good?

Now Nadia rises.

"Why don't you two go outside," she suggests. "I'll yell when it's chow time."

She looks at Blaise as she says this. Flower-bedecked, she resembles some sort of dark woods nymph rather than the woman George knows, or thinks he knows. Blaise is right. She is beautiful. He finds he is wringing his hands.

George and Blaise stand on the hill overlooking the valley, possibly in the same spot where they picnicked fifteen years ago. The apple trees are wildly thick. Everywhere, the goldenrod is waist-high, and poplar striplings are growing up taller than the children. Soon, George will have to do something about the poplars, the weeds, the rampant grass. The apple trees must be pruned, the house needs repairs. Eventually, he thinks, he will have time to do all this.

He hears himself asking, "Do you remember the picnic we had out here?"

Blaise nods, but it is clear he has no idea what George is talking about.

"You were writing a book," George tells Blaise, "about the government's dam policies. Whatever happened to that book, by the way?"

"I never got it written, George. I had a publisher, but all hell let loose out on the coast, and I never got around to it."

"I know how that is," George says.

He considers telling Blaise that his book, too, is still un-written, a novel about a love affair between two civil rights workers in the Sixties, a black girl and a white boy who meet in Mississippi, somewhat autobiographical, but he doesn't say anything.

Blaise lays an arm across George's shoulders. In friendship? Memory of friendship? On their right, over the northern range of the Blue Ridge, a storm is gathering. Clouds are piled in deepening layers of gray and silver, ominous clouds that even as George watches drift over the hump of the mountain and begin to descend into the valley. He notices that the wind has picked up and it is getting colder.

"Tell me what you're up to these days, fella," Blaise says. He does not seem to notice the approaching storm.

"Oh." George shrugs. "I teach. A couple of days a month, I hang out at the consumer clinic."

How can he explain to Blaise why he lives as he does now? Why he is not *political* anymore. Why he has chosen to be a husband and father, rather than someone who goes down to Nicaragua to talk to poets. Does he even know why himself?

Then Blaise says, "I don't know whether you were aware of this, George, but a few years ago I almost died in a motorcy-cle accident. Near San Bernardino, coming down out of the mountains."

"We heard something," George says, confused.

"I was nearly dead when they found me. Broken into pieces like Humpty Dumpty. It was a miracle they put me back to-gether again."

"Blaise, that's awful!"

George tries to imagine Blaise on the verge of death, but it is easier to see him making love. George has always imagined that Blaise was a skillful lover. Nadia has never said so, of course. They would never speak about *that*.

"Yes, George. 'Awe-ful' in its original meaning," Blaise says. "When I was dying, or thought I was dying, it was like being on an incredible high. I understood life, the universe, everything, with complete clarity. It was truly remarkable."

"Blaise, you don't know how sorry I am to hear this."

"Listen to what I'm saying, George. Almost dying was the most thrilling experience in my life."

George nods as though he understands. He doesn't, but Blaise looks at him with those piercing blue eyes as though he expects some response, some acknowledgment of the remarkable thing he has experienced: nearly dying.

At that moment, George becomes aware of Nadia standing above them on the hill. He doesn't know how long she has been there, watching them. She looks small and fragile, as though the tall grass will enclose her at any moment, devour her. He waves for her to join them and she makes her way down the hillside in her clunky sandals.

"See that?" she demands, pointing toward the storm clouds.

Her face is flushed and she breathes in little pants. At close range, Nadia does not appear at all vulnerable. She is strong, shining.

"Awesome, isn't it?" Blaise says, smiling at her.

Awe-some, George thinks. His throat tightens. Something has occurred to him. They did hear about Blaise's accident, he remembers now, and someone was on the motorcycle with him. A woman, he is certain. What happened to her? He can't remember. Blaise didn't even mention her. Why not?

"You'd better go round up the children, George," Nadia says. "We'll meet you at the house."

She is right, as usual. George salutes and she frowns. Then he heads off toward the field where the children still swing on the branches of the sugar maple. He jogs easily over the rough ground. Running is something he loves. He likes it best out here in the country. One day, he and Nadia will move out here permanently. He will fix up the farm, write a book, install cows. He hears Nadia's voice imitating his: *Cows are easy, man—*

Abruptly, he swerves and heads up to a knoll above the house. From here, he can see for miles down the valley, which at one end is drenched in golden light and at the other has turned a dark threatening purple. Directly below him, the children and Hugo romp in the field. Over to the right, Blaise and Nadia stand together in the orchard. Blaise is gesturing out over the valley.

"Fraud!" George yells into the rising wind. "Faker!"

No one hears him, of course. He shouts again, "You old bastard!"

He wants to kill the old white-headed man down there. He sees Blaise put his arm around Nadia as they start walking back up the hill to the house. "Don't touch her!" he screams, still unheard. "Take your hands off her!"

Suddenly, he is certain that a young woman is dead, tossed onto the macadam from the back of a Harley, all because of that old man. Surely that was in the article. Nadia will remember.

In the field below, little Carla is waving to him. She is wearing a white dress of some flimsy material. George waves back and starts running toward his daughter.

"Pick me up, Daddy," Carla cries, holding out her arms as he approaches.

"You can walk, sweetheart," he says, then sweeps her up and fiercely hugs her warm little body, ignoring the pain that stabs him in the back.

When the storm breaks, they are all at the table in the large paneled room, where a fire blazes in the fireplace. Everyone is ravenously eating Nadia's greens and sweet potatoes and little baked apples from the orchard. In the midst of all this good food, this warmth, this circle of family and friends, George hardly remembers the way he felt out on the mountain.

Rain thrums the roof and shakes the glass in the windows. The storm will be pent up in the valley for some time, probably all night, says Hugo, who seems to know more about these things than George and Nadia, certainly more than Blaise, who, since their walk, has seemed aloof, distracted, or, possibly, just tired.

"A great feed, Nadia!" George says. "Thank you."

Nadia lifts her eyebrows, but does not reply. He has already commented on the dinner several times. The children nudge each other and Laurel says, "Da-a-addy."

Then George remembers something else, something about Blaise's story of the woman carrying her son's head along the road in Nicaragua. George read that story in the *Washington Post* years ago. He's quite certain. He stares at Nadia. He wants to call her into the kitchen to tell her, but she is listening to Blaise with great intensity. Her face looks strained, rigid, as though something is terribly wrong.

After dinner, Hugo gets down the piñata for the children to break with sticks from the kindling basket. On closer view, the donkey is elderly, bedraggled, its blue fur shaggy, worn off in spots, soiled with suspicious-looking brown stains. The children do not notice. They leap and slash at the donkey, yelling boisterously, beside themselves with excitement. Even Carla tries. Hugo holds the donkey lower and with one of her swipes she breaks it open. Candies spill out onto the braided rug, livid pink and green things, misshapen, mottled with mold. As the children fall upon them, George and Nadia cry with one voice, "No!" "Stop!" "Don't!"

There is an instant of quiet, then melee: Carla sobs and the older children protest shrilly, while the adults try to gather up all the dreadful ruined candies. Nadia seizes the ravaged donkey, runs to the door and throws it out into the rain, a gesture so unlike Nadia—who saves even used scraps of aluminum foil—that George is stunned. He stands in the midst of this turmoil, overwhelmed with the feeling that everything is his fault.

"I'm sorry," Nadia says to Blaise. "But the candy looked so—"

"My dear," Blaise shrugs, "please don't say a word."

And Nadia goes to him and kisses him deeply on the mouth.

Later, George says, "If you just hadn't done *that*."

They are alone in their bedroom in the quiet house. George

is already in bed, while Nadia stands at the window looking out at the rain. She is wearing a long cotton nightgown, colorless from many washings. George is suddenly reminded of the time, long before the nightgown, when he asked her why she went off with Blaise. *Why?* All Nadia said was, "I wanted to."

Now, she says nothing.

"What if they'd eaten one of those rotten lumps of sugar?" he can't help saying. "And the story from *Post*—And the woman on the motorcycle—Can you believe the man?"

There is so much to deplore about Blaise that George falls back against the pillow and closes his eyes. He hears Nadia's bare feet on the floor, feels the dip of the mattress as she gets into bed.

"There's another thing," she says. Her voice is so soft he can hardly hear her. His eyes fly open. Something else?

"He doesn't remember the time he and I went off together. You know, our little jaunt."

"You talked about . . . your jaunt?"

"At dinner I mentioned it. He didn't have a clue. All he wanted to talk about was near-death experiences."

George is not surprised, though a soft pain ripens in his chest. "Same old Blaise," he says, and reaches out and strokes her arm.

With a small cry of anguish, she breaks into sobs. He takes her into his arms. He cannot remember the last time Nadia cried. *Fraud,* he thinks, furiously. *Old bastard faker!* At the same time, her grief amazes him. He had no idea she still had feelings about Blaise.

After a while, she is quiet.

He whispers, "Do you want to talk?"

"No," she murmurs and turns on her side, away from him. "Can you get the light?"

He kisses her hair, filled with love and an obscure dismay, then switches off the lamp. In the darkness, he hears the rain pounding against the side of the house. He doubts they will see Blaise Dupres again.

"Good night," he whispers. "I love you."

Nadia is silent.

The rain continues. He hears it beating on the roof, imagines it gushing in rivulets down the hill where they stood this afternoon. He wonders if they will ever move out here to the farm, as he has always planned. He listens to the rain and imagines it falling on their unpruned apple trees, falling deep into the valley and high up on the far range of dark mountains. He turns toward Nadia but does not touch her. Her breathing is scarcely audible. He stares into the darkness where she lies and thinks of the rain beating down on the donkey they have left outside, bleeding the color from its paper hide, soaking its head and body, until everything softens, dissolves, becomes something George no longer recognizes.

Heartbeatland

When Anne got home from quartet practice that afternoon, she found a little mob at her front door. Was David having a party in her absence? Doubtful. Then what were the neighbors doing on her doorstep? *The neigh-boors,* as David called them since he and Anne, *furriners* from the north, had moved to the sandy wastes of eastern North Carolina. He had made up names for all the *'boors* on their end of the block: the Widder Wilmer for the elderly widow next door; Les Boys for the couple, Bob and Eddie, in the Cape Cod on the corner; and Nessie (real name Lucinda) for the supple, long-necked yoga teacher who lived across the street. David had even given names to Anne and to himself. He was the Schoolmaster. She was the Princess Annabel.

The neighbors all turned and looked at the Princess as she pulled her Civic into the driveway behind the Schoolmaster's Jeep. So why hadn't David let them in? Was he hiding? She grinned at the image of David crouched behind the living-room sofa while the *neigh-boors* beat a tattoo on the door. At the same time, a tiny light flickered in her brain, which was still reverberating with Bartok's Fifth, the violin's eerily ascending quarter tones, the responding minor descent of the cello, the placating viola, her own anxious second violin.

Mrs. Wilmer began making her way across the sparse grass toward the car. "Hi! What's up?" Anne called, getting out of the car and letting the door slam. She noticed that the widow's face looked more than ever like a ball of dough. Anne felt her stomach knot. She flicked a piece of lint off her pullover and at the same time noted Mrs. Wilmer's plaid jacket, which was so much too big for her it must have belonged to the late Mr. Wilmer. Why wasn't the woman wearing her own coat? Anne touched her lucky silver bracelet, a present from David on her thirty-fourth birthday. Calm down, Annabel.

"Anne," Mrs. Wilmer tiptoed up to her, so close that Anne could smell her tepid Widder's breath. "David had some sort of attack. They took him to the hospital. It happened about two hours ago."

"What do you mean?" Anne demanded. "What sort of attack?"

"We don't know. He collapsed here in your driveway. Lucinda saw him from her window. He was unconscious when she got to him."

But this was ridiculous. David was in the living room, hiding behind the drapes. Anne gestured with her hands as though to shoo the Widder away and started walking toward the house, moving with unaccountable slowness as though her legs were filled with sand. Les Boys, blond muscular Bob and slim dark

Eddie, blocked her way. "He isn't here, Anne," Eddie told her, somehow divining her thoughts. "He's at the hospital. You should go there." Bob was nodding his bleached head like a windup toy. Off to the side, the yoga teacher stretched her neck beseechingly.

So Anne gave in. But even as they bundled her into her car, Bob driving, Mrs. Wilmer and Eddie in the backseat, she sensed David watching from a window of their house, holding his hand over his mouth to keep from hooting out loud at the awesome comedy of it all.

No one ever told her David was dead. She kept listening for the word, but no one ever said it. The red-haired boy intern who met them in the emergency room said merely, "I'm very sorry, Mrs. Freeman." Sorry for what, you nerd, she thought. But she couldn't say that or anything else. She could barely breathe. The Widder held onto her arm and led her to a plastic couch. "It was one of those rare sudden—" The intern's next few words were garbled. "—nothing we could do—" He shook his head as though bewildered by what had happened—*befoozled,* David would have joked, using one of his made-up words. *Dr. Red was completely befoozled.*

The specialist she met next did not mention death either. David's heart had failed, he explained. It wasn't a heart attack or a stroke, the implication being that those were solid aggressive acts of which one could be proud. What had happened to David was "failure." Outraged, Anne wanted to scratch the specialist's large, pale, cratered face. *Dr. Moon,* David might have called him.

"We believe his heart may have been weak for a long time, Mrs. Freeman. Did he often complain of fatigue?"

"Never," she said, which wasn't true. David had always required more rest than she did and was often lethargic. There had been health problems in adolescence though she couldn't remember what David had said the problems were. They had met in graduate school four years ago, when he was twenty-eight, she two years older.

"What exactly happened?" she demanded of Dr. Moon.

"We'll need to do an autopsy and even then we might not find the precise pathology."

"But you're sure—" she began, then stopped.

The flesh of the doctor's big moon face rippled. "You may see him, Mrs. Freeman. He's in the next room."

See him? See David? In the next room? Now it was she who was befoozled, struck dumb by a monstrous joke.

"I'll go in with you if you want, Anne," Mrs. Wilmer said, putting her hand on Anne's arm.

The doctor nodded his large head. Both he and the Widder made movements of rising, but the image of David lying on a table *in the next room* struck Anne with terror. Were his eyes open or shut? Was he dressed or naked under a sheet? Were his small limbs arranged in that formal way of funeral homes or were they sprawled any old way? She heard the soothing baritone of the doctor explaining that there were no disfiguring marks, that David had not suffered, and the cajoling high notes of the Widder saying she was sure Anne would be glad later that she had seen him. Then her own shrill voice rose above the others in a crescendo of despair: "No! No! I can't! I can't!"

It really got hilarious then, David, she reported, several hours later, when she was home at last, lying on their bed, a damp washcloth over her eyes. *Dr. Moon kept going, I think Mrs. Free-man would like to get on home now* (get on home!), *and the Widder kept going, yes, yes. But I wouldn't budge, David. I sat there looking at the pictures on the doctor's desk—three moon-faced teenaged girls and a peroxided wife. The Family Moon. Then he wanted to give me a pill. Now, Mrs. Freeman, if you'll just open your mouth and take this. I pretended I was a prisoner in a mental hospital and kept the tablet under my tongue. Then I said I had to go to the bathroom and I spit the pill into the toilet—*

None of it had happened that way. She had sobbed wildly, sitting on the doctor's sofa, her sobs eventually quieting, and after a while, she docilely took the sedative Dr. Moon offered with water from a paper cup. But it might have been the way she described the scene to David; her tale was an imaginative extension of reality, as David always said when they were de-constructing some dreadful dinner party, where his jokes had been met with mute stares and Anne had said hardly a word, or after a visit to The Parents, his or hers, equally dire. *Oh David, you should have seen it! You should have been there!*

During the next few days, she kept up a running account of events for David, including the arrival of their shocked and grieving parents *(I think your mother believes I did it—)* and the phone calls from stunned friends in various parts of the coun-try *(Freddie Harrell called from L.A. Remember him? The post-modern man who hated your eighteenth-century guts? He was in tears—).* She described the proliferation of chicken salads and Jell-O molds in the kitchen *(It's Tupperware city in there,*

David), while the rest of the house reeked of lilies and roses. The *neigh-boors* were tireless, serving food and hot coffee, picking up relatives at the airport, greeting callers at the door and leading them, one by one, into the small crocus-yellow den to speak to Anne, who sat silent and limp in the one good chair. *I'm completely in their hands, David. They're having a ball.*

The Widder and Nessie kept careful records of what was brought or sent—a display of mixed flowers from the head-master of the academy where David taught, a tomato aspic ring from the chair of the English department, chicken salad rolls from the parents' association, a mammoth box of pralines from David's chess club, a wreath of chrysanthemums from Anne's chamber group, red roses from their closest grad school friends in Ann Arbor—all neatly listed in the Widder's spidery hand or Nessie's big round lettering in a padded white book provided by the funeral home. At night when she went to bed, Anne lay exhausted but sleepless, recounting silently all these details to David.

David, you'll love this. There was actually a funeral. In the Presbyterian church where we went to hear the Messiah last Christmas. The off-key trumpet, remember? Today we just had the organ and good ol' Johann Sebastian. Lots of flowers. You'd have sneezed yourself silly.

As her mother commented with satisfaction, they had a most respectable turnout. Anne herself was a little surprised at the attendance, considering the fact that she and David had lived in the town less than a year. She had not realized David was so popular at the academy; students, parents, and teachers came out in force. There was a group of women she knew from the arts center where she gave violin lessons—*the gaggle,* David called them—and some scruffy-looking men she surmised were the chess club. Of course the *neigh-boors* were there, sitting together on the fourth row. The young preacher, who had never met David, extemporized freely on his dedication to his students, his love of literature, his delightful sense of humor— describing a person, Anne assured David from her wet pillow (who was crying?), they would never have invited to dinner.

It was because she felt David's presence in the house so keenly that she decided to stay on there, at least for a while. Her parents, accustomed to Greenwich, Connecticut, were amazed that she would choose to remain, even briefly, in such a cultural desert, where there were only a half dozen movie theaters and going out to dinner meant Taco Bell. The house she and David had bought was no prize either, an elderly clapboard in a far from posh *neigh-boor*-hood. They had done a lot of work on the house, painting rooms warm reds and yellows and livening up their old furniture, chipped graduate school Danish, with pieces of kitsch they'd found in local stores—an overstuffed sofa they dubbed Moby Dick, a small corner cabinet David called a *what-for,* a wicker chair that creaked obscenely when anyone sat in it. *(Would you hush!* David would exclaim, alarming the visitor and making Anne shake with silent laughter. *Wicked wicker!)* She could not imagine leaving all this priceless junk just because David had gone into hiding.

Her mother stayed with her for a week after the funeral. During that time, Anne wrote thank-you notes and met with a lawyer who explained David's life insurance policy, which she had not known he had. She slept badly and could get down only consommé and baked potato, foods she had been given when she was sick as a child. Her mother cooked and did the shopping, and at night they sat together and watched television. They rarely mentioned David, though when another sympathy card arrived in the mail or a casserole appeared on the doorstep, her mother would shake her head in mild astonishment.

"You and David managed to make a lot of friends in a short time," she commented one evening during a commercial.

Anne was watching a shaved-head hunk guzzle a beer. She and David rarely watched TV. She'd had no idea commercials had deteriorated so drastically.

"What? Oh. David knows a lot more people than I do."

Her mother did not remark on her use of the present tense, but went on in a musing tone, "Yes, he would talk to practically anybody. Though he never said much when your father and I were around. I sometimes think I didn't know David very well."

She paused, probably waiting to see whether Anne would grow teary. But Anne kept her eyes on the guzzler, now surrounded by a bevy of babes, while a part of her brain acknowledged the truth of what her mother said: No one really knew the Schoolmaster, except the Princess.

"Maybe I should stay longer than a week," her mother said as the commercial ended, bringing Anne back to reality with a cymbal crash.

"That's not necessary, Mother. I'll be fine."

She tried to keep her voice calm, not revealing the panic she felt at the prospect of her mother's staying on. The two of them were not close, despite the fact that people often remarked on how alike they looked, both slim and dark-haired, their faces apple-shaped, their chins slightly receding. At first, her mother's presence had been a comfort, but it was hard to concentrate on David, behind the curtains, around the corner, when her mother was sitting there beside her.

"Daddy'll starve if you don't go home," she added firmly.

"Well," her mother said, which Anne knew meant she agreed. A great many of their conversations ended with that sad long-note: *Well.*

The night before her mother left, they invited the neighbors over for dessert and coffee as a way of thanking them for all they had done. Anne's mother served apple strudel. Anne played David's favorite CDs, Mozart's third horn concerto, a medley of Gregorian chants, the Stones. Everyone talked about inoffensive topics such as the weather—spring was near, someone had seen a first crocus. Only one wrong note was struck when Bob, the more aggressive of Les Boys, asked her what she was going to do with David's Jeep.

"What do you mean?" she asked.

"You're going to sell it, aren't you?" Bob asked, speaking slowly and carefully, as though she were retarded.

She stared at him coldly, noting his prominent pecs, his blond buzz. Bob worked in an office supply store. His partner, Eddie, who reminded Anne's mother of Montgomery Clift, was unemployed. The two of them planned to open a home decorating business as soon as they could scrape up the money.

"I don't know what I'm going to do with the Jeep," she answered, also speaking slowly to show she would not be intimidated. "Maybe I'll drive it."

"You don't need two cars," Bob retorted, angering her further.

"I'm sorry, Bob. I'm not ready to think about cars yet."

The others were looking at them and Bob sullenly subsided.

The next morning when Anne drove her mother to the airport, she took the Jeep just to show Bob.

Instead of the relief she expected after her mother's departure, Anne found that she no longer had the impulse to tell David what was happening, perhaps because nothing was. She would not go back to teaching for another week, people had stopped dropping by, and she did not expect anyone to call, except possibly her friend Elizabeth, the first violinist in the quartet. The Widder might come over to check on her. Nessie might pop in. Or they might not. She wasn't familiar with the shelf life of sympathy. What was she supposed to do now? She noticed a sinister *hmmmm* in the percussion section of her brain, underlying the massive silence of the house. *Okay, David, enough's enough. Joke's over. Come out, come out, wherever you are. Oh David. Where* are *you?* When she went to bed, the muted rumble of kettle drums grew louder, filling her head, blocking her ears and nasal passages. She had never imagined that grief felt like flu.

A few days later, slightly more energetic, she invited Nessie— oops! Lucinda—over for tea. Nessie had been the one to find David and call the rescue squad and Anne felt she owed more to her than to anyone else. The yoga teacher arrived wearing a black leotard and a jeans shirt tied at the waist. She sat down on Anne's sofa and folded her legs Indian fashion, right foot on left thigh, torso straight. Would weirdness never cease! David would get a kick out of hearing how Nessie sat. Having something to tell him made her feel better.

"I'm curious, Lucinda," Anne said, reminding herself not to call her Nessie. "How did you happen to notice David that day? I hope you don't mind my asking."

"I don't mind," Lucinda responded so promptly Anne was taken aback. "What happened was I was waiting for a new client to show. Tulip Street's not exactly the center of the universe. People always get lost trying to find it. So I was looking out the window and I saw David walking down the street toward your house. I didn't think anything about it. He looked—"

"Excuse me," Anne interrupted. "You say he was walking toward our house?"

"He'd been at Bob and Eddie's. I thought you knew that."

Anne had not known. David never visited Bob and Eddie, at least not that she knew of. In her brain she heard the warning slide of an oboe.

"He must have gone over there to borrow something," she heard herself say. "Bob's got all those tools."

Lucinda swayed forward and patted Anne's knee. "David was a people person, honey. He liked everybody."

Anne bristled. Nessie had no right to lecture her on what David was like. She felt confused, *befoozled*. She poured more of the herbal tea she had bought especially for today and passed the plate of brownies Mrs. Wilmer had dropped off that morning. She asked Nessie about her yoga classes, expressing an interest she in no way felt. Soon Nessie went home, leaving Anne nervous and agitated. She was probably being a *silly-filly*, as David would say when she worried, but it seemed odd that David had been visiting Bob and Eddie just before his attack. Why? And nobody had said anything about it. Why not?

She woke the next morning with a headache she knew would remain with her all day. Nonetheless, after breakfast she walked down the street to return the Jemima Puddleduck plate on which Mrs. Wilmer had delivered the brownies.

"They were delicious. I scarfed them all with a little help from Lucinda."

Mrs. Wilmer looked puzzled but did not inquire what "scarf" meant.

"By the way, Mrs. Wilmer," Anne paused, glancing around the Widder's all-stainless kitchen, a Fifties museum piece that had driven David into ecstasies when he first saw it. "Did you know David was at Bob and Eddie's just before he collapsed?"

Mrs. Wilmer had not known. She'd been reading the paper when she heard the ambulance.

"And Bob and Eddie?" Anne asked. "Were they alerted by the siren too?"

"I believe," the Widder said in her tentative way, "they were already on the scene."

That afternoon Anne called Eddie, knowing Bob was at work, and asked if David had borrowed a wrench from them. She had found one, she said, and thought it might be theirs. She told the lie effortlessly. She didn't even know what a wrench looked like.

Eddie didn't remember David's borrowing anything.

"But listen, Anne," he said, "have you given any more thought to the Jeep? Our offer's still good."

"No, I haven't, Eddie." She pictured him coyly regarding the telephone with his warm puppy eyes, a lock of dark hair falling over his forehead.

"Bob's truck is on its last legs," Eddie said.

Block that metaphor, she heard David chortle.

"There goes my kettle, Eddie. Talk to you later."

On Monday she returned to her violin classes at the arts center. Her friends—*the gaggle*—marveled at her recovery. "You're so strong, Anne," Sybil MacInturff gushed. "I know I could never come back to work so soon if Randy—I mean, I just couldn't. I would look like a *freak.*" How like Sybil to worry about how she would look as a grieving widow, Anne thought. Yet she knew Sybil meant to be kind.

Anne had lost weight and was pale as a ghost, but since she was naturally slender and fair-skinned, people did not seem to notice a difference. She still could not eat much besides soup and baked potato, and although she managed her classes and resumed practicing the violin in the evenings, the nights were torture. She lay awake thinking awful thoughts and when she slept, she dreamed awful dreams, herself being chased by dogs, her mother lying dead on a table, a great moon crushing her.

David, what were you doing at Eddie and Bob's?

Other questions nagged her. There was that girl at the funeral whom Anne had never seen before, a chunky young woman standing at the edge of the crowd at the cemetery, ferociously biting her lower lip. Maybe she worked at a store where David shopped. David often chatted in checkout lines, entertaining people with his leprechaun charm. She was intrigued by the thought that a checkout girl had a crush on David. She did not for a moment believe David had been attracted by *her*.

A dissonant chord kept sounding in her brain. How well did she really know David? She had always talked to him about what bothered her, her resentment of her remote parents, her guilt at neglecting her music, her shyness. David seemed genuinely interested in her problems and never failed to respond with reassurance, but he had rarely talked about problems of his own. Most of the time, they had conversed in a witty banter, literary, acerbic. They liked to mock people, even those closest to them, even themselves. She wondered about this habit now.

And on top of everything, Bob had left two messages on her answering machine, saying he wanted to talk to her about David's car. She did not return the calls.

She had been back teaching for a week when Eddie phoned and invited her to dinner. "Just us," he said, meaning him and Bob. "We want you to see our house."

The real reason, she knew, was the Jeep, still sitting in her driveway, undriven since her mother left—she'd never felt safe with those canvas sides. Her inclination was to refuse but, drawing a deep breath, she forced herself to say she'd come. She had never been inside Bob and Eddie's house. According to Nessie it was decorated to the max, which Nessie meant as a compliment. Anne imagined small rooms crammed with flowered chintz, windows sheathed in matching valances, lozenge-shaped rugs lying treacherously on oiled pine floors. She thought if she saw the house and told David about it afterward, they would have a good laugh and put an end to her wondering.

On Friday at six-thirty, she walked slowly down the street carrying a bottle of red wine. It was a mild April evening. Nessie was in her yard picking tulips. Anne waved and Nessie waved back. Next, Anne waved to Mrs. Wilmer, who was doing something on her porch, and the Widder waved back. The *neighboors*. She smiled and at the same time her eyes stung with useless tears. She had nothing in common with these people and yet they had come to her aid when she needed them. Now she felt saddled with them, yet grateful, too. How strange.

Eddie greeted her with a hug and invited her in. She stood still in shock, gazing at an expanse of black tile and white walls, leather and chrome, everything black or tan with dashes of white. *It's gorgeous,* she would tell David, *if you like S & M.*

"Wow," she said aloud.

Eddie smiled as though he'd expected her surprise.

"Bob'll be with us in a minute. He got home late because the truck broke down. Again."

Ah, the opening salvo in the car war. Anne ignored it and asked if he would show her around.

"We're into houses, Anne, but some people could care less about interior decor. You know what I mean?"

She did know. She insisted on a tour anyway. The whole thing didn't take long since walls had been eliminated and practically the whole first floor could be seen at a glance— living-dining-room divided by a counter from state-of-the-art kitchen. There was also a luxurious purple powder room, a redwood deck out back, and a master bedroom upstairs, which they skipped because Bob was changing.

Last, Eddie took her down to the basement to show her a black-painted room fitted out with a bar, elaborate stereo system, and giant television screen.

"David would have loved that," she said, pointing to the humongous screen, knowing David would have ridiculed it unmercifully.

"Oh he did!" Eddie responded.

He did?

"He saw it?" she asked. "He was here?"

"Oh yes. Several times. You were off with your music group I think."

Eddie looked expectant. Anne said nothing.

"He used to come over and tell us his teacher stories. He would *regale* us. Dave was so funny. I could listen to him forever."

Dave—

"I hear Bob." Eddie ran to the stairs. "We're in the rec room, Bobby."

Bob appeared wearing jeans and a tight black T-shirt, carrying a can of beer. He looked scrubbed, obscenely clean. Anne shuddered.

"Anne and I were just talking about what a good storyteller Dave was," Eddie said.

Bob nodded. "A real fun guy. He could have had a career as a stand-up."

Anne felt sick at the thought. She said weakly, "Someone said he was over here just before he had his attack."

"Yeah?" Bob looked at her with his mean little eyes.

"He was here." Eddie responded quickly as though to cover Bob's rudeness. "He looked a little tired. I remember he said he was going home to take a nap."

There was a pause during which she could hear her heart's syncopated beat, th-thump, th-thump. Surely they could hear it, too.

"Dave was a great guy, Anne," Eddie said, casting a look at the silent Bob. "We loved him dearly. Now. Let's go upstairs and give *you* a glass of wine and let *me* do the *au jus.*"

He pronounced it "oh juice," but Anne barely registered the fact. *Dave.* Telling them his teacher stories. *Regaling.* She wanted urgently to leave. Whatever she might learn from Bob and Eddie about *Dave,* she didn't want to hear it. But she climbed the stairs to the living room and sank into a black Naugahyde chair and accepted a glass of red wine in a stemmed crystal glass. She leaned her head back in the chair and pretended to listen to Bob's account of his breakdown on I-95 that afternoon. She finished her wine and let Bob refill her glass. She heard him say his carburetor was gone, that AAA had taken two hours to send a tow. Oh—was that Mozart on the stereo? Yes, it was.

At dinner, served on a glass slab set on steel pylons, she drank more wine and was surprised that it seemed to make her exceptionally clear-headed. She noticed every detail of the meal, the rice pilaf sprinkled with parsley, the fresh asparagus with lemon, the rack of lamb "oh juice." She noted Bob's churlishness as he asked for a slice of *cooked* meat. Out of habit she recorded it all to tell David later, except that David already *knew* and had never told her.

"I need to talk to you, Anne," Bob said, showing his small sharp teeth.

Here it comes, she thought.

"My truck's dead. Deader'n a doornail—"

"What? What did you say?" There it was! The word nobody would say. She felt her face blaze.

"What did I say?" Bob inquired of Eddie, who rolled his large liquid eyes.

"It's all right," Anne said. "I don't mind."

They both stared at her. She took a bite of her salad. Perhaps the wine had affected her after all.

"I'll give you five thousand," Bob said.

She swallowed. "Bob, I'm not going to sell the Jeep just yet. And that price strikes me as laughably low."

"What did David pay for it?" he asked stonily.

"I don't remember."

"You have the sale papers?"

"I have no idea. I don't want to talk about this, Bob."

"They're asking a couple thousand to fix the truck. Anne, I think David would have wanted us to have the Jeep."

She had *known* Bob would say something like that, insinuating something that wasn't true, but which having been insinuated would assume a life of its own, causing her to second-guess everything, her and David, David himself, dear antic David. *Dave.* She put down her fork, all clear-headedness gone.

"I think I've drunk too much wine. It's my own fault and I'm sorry, but I'm going to have to go home."

Her voice was calm and clear. She felt reassured to hear it in this strange room.

"Oh don't *go*," Eddie wailed. "I've made tiramisu."

Whatever that was. "It was a wonderful meal, Eddie," she said. "Truly. But I'm going to have to go home and lie down."

"I'll walk you," Bob said and got up.

She protested but he went with her anyway. They walked down the dark street in silence. As they were passing the Widder's house he began to whistle. Beethoven's Eighth? The Beatles? Before her brain could sort out the melody, he stopped whistling and put his hands in his pockets. Anne concentrated on the little beacon that was the lamp she had left on in her living room, but a piccolo trill in her brain made her glance at Bob, walking beside her, his hair glowing as though dipped in whatever they put on clock dials to make them shine. He too seemed to be looking at the lighted window. Did he see David peeking out with an elfin grin? No. He was looking at the Jeep in the driveway. Oh lord. *What'll I do, David? He hates my guts and he wants your car.* Then they were at her door. "Good night. Thanks again," she murmured and rushed inside, hoping he'd think she was about to be sick.

The next day, unable to throw off a fatigue so dire she had to cancel her classes, she phoned a therapist whose card Elizabeth had forced upon her. Anne had intended to tear it up—how *could* Elizabeth?—but it was somehow still there among the clutter of condolence notes on the hall table, the card perhaps a condolence, too. How many times had she and David ridiculed therapists and the bromides they offered? Now, however, fighting another headache, fighting panic at the thought of Bob and the car, fighting yet another inundation of tears, Anne grimly picked up the phone. She would not tell the therapist everything, of course. And if he was prying or rude, she would simply never go back.

Dr. Booth turned out to be a thick-necked middle-aged man who looked like someone she would do her best to avoid at a party—too earnest, not a joke in him. It didn't matter what he was like, as it turned out. She began to cry the instant she sat down on his hard tweed sofa and continued to sob for the next fifty minutes. Dr. Booth never said a word, or not that she noticed. At the second session, she did not cry, nor did she speak. Her throat was frozen. Dr. Booth kept up a genial patter about the stages of grief and other nonsense while she listened, numb, drained, a zombie. *Dr. Trooth, David. I am seeing a Dr. Trooth.*

The third week, she told Dr. Booth, at his suggestion (he was a "talking" shrink), how she had felt on each day leading up to her appointment. Monday was a good day; she'd read the newspaper and made lesson plans. Tuesday she'd had trouble getting out of bed. Wednesday she was a wreck and cried for half an hour in the ladies' room at the arts center. That morning, Thursday, she'd thrown up her breakfast. Dr. Booth did not seem surprised at her reports, which annoyed her.

The fourth Thursday, she found herself describing a dream she had had, a horrible dream to do with wrenches and hammers and great violence done to her person. The next thing she knew, with no segue at all, she was describing David, how he had grown up in West Orange, New Jersey, and graduated from Yale, which he attended on scholarship; how he liked good clothes, which may have been due to his father's owning a men's clothing store; how he had earned a PhD in English literature at the University of Michigan, where'd they met in a class on Restoration drama. (She was getting a degree in education.) Sitting in adjacent desks, they'd played tic-tac-toe during the professor's boring lectures. Neither won a single game from the other the entire semester.

"What does that tell you?" she asked, challengingly.

Dr. Booth blinked his round eyes: *be-foozled.*

She went on describing their mute exchanges in reaction to some foolish thing the professor said—David's lifted eyebrow, her curled lip. Soon they were walking together to the cafeteria for lunch, meeting at the *Rats-killer* for dinner. The relief in talking about all this was so profound she slept soundly that night for the first time since the event she still thought of as "David's joke."

May arrived—the azaleas were in full electric bloom—and she became used to driving to the plain brick bungalow every Thursday afternoon, taking the path around the side of the house to a door that opened into a basement waiting room stocked with plaid furniture and years-old *National Geographics.* She sat gazing at pictures of Arctic seals and Tibetan yak drovers until a person she never looked at passed silently through the room and out the door and it was her turn. *What do you guess Dr. Trooth looks like, David? Gray beard and specs? Wrong! He's bald and has a little round belly that shakes when he laughs like—* Though the therapist never laughed. Occasionally, he smiled, a gentle upturning of the lips that was almost like a caress.

As the weeks passed, she talked to Dr. Booth with increasing freedom and something like enjoyment. She didn't tell him everything. She didn't tell him about Bob and Eddie or the car or her obsession with David's secret life, which continued to occupy her mind, just as Bob continued to bully her about the Jeep. Once or twice a week he left a message on her phone machine. "Why don't you call me back, Anne? You think I'm gonna bite or something?" He had upped his offer to six thousand, which the Jeep wasn't worth according to the blue book value she had gone to the trouble to look up. He seemed irrationally determined to have the damned car. *Why, David?*

One afternoon she saw the Widder Wilmer cutting roses in her yard and walked over.

"Mrs. Wilmer, I have a problem."

She explained Bob's desire to buy the Jeep and added, "I'm not ready to sell it to anyone yet. But when I do, I'm not sure I want to sell it to Bob and Eddie. David didn't much care for those boys."

She paused, hoping the Widder would shed some light even if it was unwelcome. *What do you mean, Anne? David was always over at Bob and Eddie's. They were great pals.*

But all the Widder said was, "What's Bob offering?"

"Tell me," Dr. Booth said one Thursday, in his friendly naive way. "How was sex with you two?"

She had been seeing him for two months and actually looked forward to their "trysts," as she called them to shock her friend Elizabeth. That particular day she planned to bring up the question of whether she would stay in town for another year. The arts center had offered her more classes in the fall. She was about to launch into the topic when he threw this bolt out of the blue.

"Sex?"

"That's right. Was it good?" Dr. Booth asked.

Oh really! She suspected this was his inept way of getting her to dig deeper into her feelings. Often she felt they were skimming the surface and she tended to put the blame on Dr. Booth. He was the professional, not she. But sex? What was there to tell?

"Listen," she said, speaking sternly so as to put the matter to rest. "I loved David. We had fun together. We joked a lot."

"So sex was good," he said.

Of course sex was not good. They were both embarrassed, clumsy, too inside their heads to enjoy each other's bodies. She remembered, reluctantly, how they had begun to make love a few months after they met. The drama class had ended and they were spending more time at David's apartment. Inevitably the moment came when David kissed her, a dry pressing of lips that left them both so unnerved there was nothing to do but kiss again, until, thankfully, the CD ended and David scurried off to insert another. But gradually they had gained confidence. It was after an unexpectedly pleasurable afternoon of lovemaking on a down comforter on David's living-room floor that he said, "Can you imagine us getting married?" She had thought it was another of his fantasy riffs—*Can you imagine us parachuting off the Empire State Building?*—and responded with a throaty giggle. She was shocked when she realized he wasn't giggling along with her; he was weeping, his small white body curled beside her, his hands over his face. She'd felt ashamed to the roots of her hair.

When he calmed down he asked her to leave, but she refused. She stayed even when he locked himself in the bath-room. She dressed and smoothed out the wrinkles in the rug. After a while, she heard the bathroom door open and, a few seconds later, the bedroom door close. Still she remained sit-ting on the sofa with her hands in her lap, staring at the wall opposite, at the delicate peach-color paint David had chosen, while the minute hand on the mantelpiece clock performed one round and started another. She knew if she left, she would never see him again.

She was beginning to fear David had harmed himself when he shuffled into the room, wearing, unaccountably, a ski cap and muffler. He looked like an old man. He sat down beside her on the sofa and, when he said nothing, she began to talk. She told him about her disastrous romantic history, the inap-propriate men she had fallen for, handsome but oafish or un-kind, the humiliation she felt when whatever happened with one of them was over, her despair when she turned thirty with-out knowing love. At this point, David reached for her hand. It took a long time, but at last she was able to convince him that she *could* imagine marrying him.

Their sexual enthusiasm, if that was what it was, waned af-ter the wedding in her parents' house in Greenwich. They slept and read during most of the honeymoon, a rainy week at an inn on the Bay of Fundy. By the time David had his degree and they moved to "the wasteland," sex was practically nonexistent, unless you counted cuddling on the sofa under an afghan while watching *Star Trek* reruns or a rental movie. Yes, she'd worried at times; words like "normal" had drifted through her mind ("normal" being one of her mother's favorite concepts), but in fact, she found the absence of sex a relief. She had never figured out what all the fuss was about, and she was fairly sure David felt the same way. Wasn't that diffidence one of their affinities?

Dr. Booth didn't need to know all of these details. "We weren't very experienced," she offered. "At least I wasn't and I'm pretty sure David wasn't either."

The doctor waited, a patient stillness on his bovine face. Anne began at that moment to hate him. This session would be their last. Was it this lightning decision that made her say what she said next?

"I think David may have been gay."

Had she ever had this thought before? No, *never.* But yes, she *had.*

Dr. Booth's head tilted slightly, his voice was calm. "Why do you think so?"

"Well," she forced herself to continue, "he didn't really like sex with me. I think he initiated it, when he did, because he thought I expected it. Maybe he expected it, too. We didn't make love often."

"How often?"

"Oh really!" Anne couldn't restrain herself. She felt heartsick, soiled.

"Once a week?" he prompted, undeterred. What a jerk.

"Maybe once a month. I didn't keep track." (Though she had.)

"Ah."

"What does 'ah' mean? How often do you and Mrs. Booth have sex? Huh?"

He had the nerve to smile.

"Fuck you," she yelled, goaded into using a word that had never before passed her lips. "You've ruined everything."

Oh David, David, I've betrayed you. She had never cried so bitterly, not even at the hospital. Yet, oddly, she left the office with a lighter heart. True, she looked a wreck. (What would Sybil MacInturff say if she saw her?) But she felt, well, lighter. Her and David's sex life, or non-sex life, had been a blot on an otherwise bright tapestry. Now that blot seemed smaller, or conversely, the colors around it were several shades richer. She had loved their marriage as much as she loved David. Was that normal? Not normal? Who cared?

Later, curled on the sofa, a Brahms piano concerto on the stereo, she explained her feelings to David in a voice that was new to her—no banter, no sarcasm—but a voice she trusted, a little like Dr. Booth's. Her angst had lessened, she told him. She felt—how to say this?—as though her heart were under glass. *It's not unpleasant, David. It may be a little like being dead.*

The next day, when Anne got home from the arts center, she saw the Widder and Nessie standing in front of Les Boys' house, gabbing. They waved when they saw her, then turned back to their conversation. They seemed surprised when she walked down and joined them.

"Hi, Anne. How are you, sweetie?" asked Nessie.

"You look perky," the Widder commented.

"I feel better," Anne said and added coyly, "I'm seeing someone."

The widow frowned and Nessie's green eyes clouded over.

"A doctor," Anne added, ashamed of her little joke. "A thera-pist actually. He's helping me a lot."

Their faces cleared.

"That's so good," Nessie said.

"If it helps," the Widder added.

"You know, Anne," Mrs. Wilmer went on, "a month or two after Henry died, I baked cookies all one day. I started baking 'em after breakfast and kept going until suppertime, batch after batch after batch. Only reason I stopped was I ran out of flour. Musta baked a couple thousand."

"Oatmeal with raisins," Nessie murmured. "Sugar cookies and gingersnaps."

Mrs. Wilmer continued recalling her cookie bender, the ache in her arms from rolling dough, the sugary smell that suffused the house for weeks. "Felt a lot better after that," she wound up, taking a handkerchief out of her sleeve and blowing her nose.

Nessie reached out and placed her palm against Anne's cheek. "I've gotta run, sweetie. You take care."

"What time is it?" the Widder chimed. "I have a shoulder in the oven."

A shoulder in the oven—Anne noted the phrase, but did not remind herself to repeat it to David.

After they left, she stood in the street and gazed at Bob and Eddie's house, the gray siding, the concrete walk lined with blue hydrangeas, the red-painted door. *I'm probably being silly,* she would begin.

She walked up to the door and knocked.

"Hi, Anne." Eddie did not seem surprised to see her. Behind

him, she glimpsed a bristle of yellow hair over the rim of the Naugahyde chair.

"Eddie, I want to say two things," she said. "First, I've decided to let Bob buy David's Jeep."

Eddie's upper lip twitched. "What's the other thing?"

She steadied herself on the door frame. "I want to explain my attitude about the car. After David died—" There! She'd said the word.

"Who's that, Ed?" she heard Bob call.

"It's Anne," Eddie called back. "She's changed her mind about the Jeep."

"I'll take five thousand," Anne yelled.

The blond bristle quivered. Bob stood up. As he sauntered toward them, he and Eddie exchanged glances.

Bob said, "I guess you didn't notice what's parked in front of our house."

Anne whirled around. At the curb—how could she not have noticed?—was parked an enormous black SUV.

Was this some sort of joke?

"Is that car yours?" Anne asked.

"Bought the beast today," Bob said. "Mortgaged the house for her. Gotta thank you, Anne, for forcing us to think bi-i-ig."

Anne felt dizzy.

"Well," she said.

David, you've been ditched for a monster.

"You want to come in, Anne?" Eddie asked. "I just made lemonade."

Anne shook her head, trying to think. She would put an ad

in the paper. She would ask four thousand. A bargain for the Jeep. Tears began to rise.

Bob and Eddie stood in the doorway gazing at her.

"You know, I'm probably being silly," she began, then stopped. No, she wouldn't go there. To hell with her fears and wonderings. Les Boys were people. The Schoolmaster was a people person. Princess Annabel was a mess.

At home, she lowered herself onto Moby Dick's gray-white bulk and slipped off her shoes. Her body felt stiff and unused, but her mind pulsed with a hypnotic Philip Glass–like rhythm, a sign of something: perhaps she was ready to move on. She thought of Bob and Eddie. What would they have said if she'd told them about her anxieties? They might have looked at her as though she'd lost her mind, but no—perhaps Bob would have confessed that he had fallen for David, causing Eddie to freak out, and Eddie might have interrupted to assure her that David didn't know; he'd had no part in their emotional turmoil but merely enjoyed entertaining them with his stand-up routines. *The Schoolmaster loved Princess Annabel.*

"I love you, too," she whispered as she wept.

And there was David, his fair hair, his urchin's grin. It was to be her final vision of him in his early afterlife, but she did not know that yet. He was beside her when she finally closed her eyes and slept. When she woke, the room was empty. She thought she saw one of the drapes twitch. She looked again; it hung heavy and still.

Queen of the May

∽

It was spring again and nothing had changed, except that Carolyn had put on more weight. The extra flesh padded her thighs with a soft silkiness, and her upper arms felt pillowy where they touched her breasts, as though she wore a life jacket that was permanently attached. Sometimes when she walked she had the feeling of floating, though she wasn't really that huge—a size sixteen the last time she stopped at Razook's and the saleswoman showed her a purple muumuu and praised her "mature figure." But her face was still hers. There, in the blue eyes and ever-so-slightly-tipped nose and petal-like lips, she could discover the girl who had been her college's May Queen twenty years ago and danced barefoot on the grass with her court, slender pretty girls all laughing and glancing brightly at the crowd of onlookers, fathers and mothers and boyfriends riotously applauding.

The extra weight made dancing less desirable now, even if there had been the opportunity. In all ways, she seemed to move more slowly through her days, which was why, this morning, the yardman caught her still sitting at the breakfast table in her yellow robe. He was a county boy named Alan Turner who had worked for her the summer before. She had looked forward to his coming back in spring.

"Didn' scare you, did I, Miz Martin?"

He stretched one arm up and propped it against the doorjamb. He was lean-limbed and narrow-hipped. A Confederate flag bandanna held back his long, mud-colored hair.

"Well, yes, you did a little, Alan." She smiled and peeped at the bright fur in his armpit.

"You didn' hear the truck?"

"I didn't hear a thing." A lie: his truck would wake the dead. "Don't tell me it's time to mow already."

"Nope," he said. "Time to seed."

They both turned and looked out the window at her large troublesome lawn, a broad pine-studded swath of patchy grass straggling down to a small lake. The lake was communally owned by the residents of Wilde Woode Estates, an exclusive development of a dozen houses out in the middle of nowhere in piney, sandy eastern North Carolina. All the houses had enormous yards, but it was hard to grow grass in any of them. Only bushes and weeds did well, though Alan had tried. Azaleas ran along two sides of the yard, their leaves still dark, no hint of the pink and scarlet glory to come. Little crowds of daffodils bloomed against the fence and, down near the lake, the forsythia had produced the first of its sunny yellow fronds.

"Everything seems to be coming out early this year," she said. "Or is it just me?"

"It's that warm winter we had. Dogwood and redbud gonna pop at the same time. You don't see that too often."

He pronounced the word "of-ten," the way county people did. Alan lived in a community called Sandspur, a collection of small houses and trailer homes hugging the road halfway between Wilde Woode and the town of Carthage. She had driven past those houses a million times without dreaming they actually had a name until Alan mentioned it last summer: Sandspur. One of the houses, a blue frame, sported a sign, "Sharon's Beauty Saloon," that made her smile every time she passed it. Alan lived in a trailer. His wife's name was Melody.

"There're some worn spots down by the fence," she said, thinking of Melody but not wanting to ask about her yet. Melody drove Alan crazy with her smoking and other self-destructive habits.

"I seen 'em," he said, meaning the grassless spots. "I'm gonna start down there. I'll stake off the places I seed so nobody'll walk on 'em."

"Oh, don't bother staking. Nobody walks out here but me."

She gave a little laugh. It wasn't a convivial neighborhood. Everybody residing in Wilde Woode, except her, left every morning to go to work in Carthage or else stayed home behind closed drapes all day. Even on weekends she rarely saw neighbors out in their yards. It was a lonely existence for someone used to living in town with friends running in and out and a hectic schedule of club meetings, PTA, and church events, most of which she had had to drop since they moved out here, though maybe *had to* was too strong; she just *had.* Her husband, John, the one who'd said he wanted a little peace and quiet when he came home, was hardly ever at home. And their children seemed to have evaporated overnight. Her son was at Carolina now and her daughter was off in the Richmond girls' school Carolyn herself had attended.

"Well, I guess I'd better get dressed," she said, glancing down at her large ruffled front. She wished Alan would go on out in the yard before she had to stand up, though perhaps it was vain of her to think he would notice how much heavier she had become. But Alan didn't show signs of going outside yet. He was digging something out of the pocket of his jeans.

"You remember that project we talked about last summer, Miz Martin? Have you given any more thought to that?" He spread a wrinkled sheet of paper on the table in front of her. "Here you go. I drew a picture."

She gave a little cry. "The gazebo! I'd forgotten all about that."

Another lie: She had thought often about the gazebo. It was an idea she and Alan dreamed up one day last summer during one of their rambling talks when she had brought a pitcher of iced tea out to where he was working on the lawn—actually a whole tray with lemon, fresh mint, cookies. She couldn't remember which of them had first suggested a summerhouse, and it didn't matter. The idea excited them both. She had mentioned it to her mother-in-law, who said that if Carolyn wanted such a contraption, by golly, she ought to have one. Carolyn had not yet broached the idea to John.

At first, she couldn't make head or tail of Alan's sketch. Then an elongated figure took shape in the maze of pencil lines, as in one of those paper placemats in restaurants catering to children: *Find the bunny rabbit and the bicycle.* This figure resembled a birdcage.

"What d'you think?" Alan demanded.

"I love the way you've drawn the roof. Like a circus tent." (But really like a cage. What better for her?) "What's all this?" She pointed to an explosion of tiny lines at the top of the drawing.

"Decoration. We can leave it off if you want."

"Let me think about it. Could you build this by yourself, Alan?"

"Sure. I could do it next week."

"It's very tempting. I'll have to talk to my husband though. May I keep this?" She picked up the paper. "You go on and start. I'm supposed to play golf with my mother-in-law, but I should be back before you leave."

Oh why didn't he go on out in the yard before she had to stand up?

"You mind if I get some coffee, Miz Martin? I saw you had your pot plugged in."

"Help yourself. You know where the cups are."

Relieved, she waited until he disappeared into the kitchen, then heaved out of her chair and pushed through the swinging door into the dining room.

The dining room was her least favorite room in the house, mainly because it was so rarely used, despite the mahogany table that seated twelve and the matching chairs covered in Italian silk. The only thing she really liked in the room was the silver service on the buffet. Her mother-in-law had given it to them on their anniversary ten years ago. "Here. *You* polish it," Peggy

Martin had said, as though she were passing on a family curse. "Just throw it all in the bathtub. That's the easiest way to do silver." But Carolyn didn't mind taking care of the silver. Twice a year, she spread newspapers over the breakfast table and sat down with several jars of polish and a pile of John's old undershirts. By the time she finished, the silver service and the candelabra and all the useless coasters and candy dishes gleamed bright as stars, taking her back to her old self, the sylph who had danced around the table laden with wedding gifts for her and John, so happy, expecting so much from life.

Beyond the dining room was the front hall and on the other side of the hall, a vast pastel living room packed with sofas and chairs in various seating arrangements, one facing the fireplace, another in a window alcove looking out over the lake. Her mother-in-law claimed the living room beat anything she'd ever seen in *House & Garden.* In addition to everything else, there was a Japanese screen their decorator had found in Raleigh and a baby grand nobody played. Her daughter had taken lessons for a few years and Carolyn could plunk out hymns, but lately she hadn't even bothered to have it tuned. Because of the unused piano, she didn't like the living room much anymore either.

As she passed through the hall and started up the stairs, she heard the back door slam, which meant Alan must be taking his coffee outside. If she hadn't made this golf date with Peggy, she could have spent the whole morning working in the yard with Alan. The day was warm with just the hint of a breeze spiced with the winey odor of pine sap. No bugs yet. Alan would have told her about Melody and their arguments over her many trips to the Kwik-Pick to buy cigarettes and about his dream of moving to California to tend the yards of movie stars. She loved hearing his stories and his dreams, all so different from her own, so much more imaginative. Last summer her girlfriends had asked her why they didn't see her more often in town and she had replied coyly that she was spending time with her yardman. The girls got a hoot out of that.

But she could not disappoint her mother-in-law. Though it was still early, Peggy would already be dressed in her plaid golf skirt and Lacrosse shirt that made her look like a little girl of six, with her tiny body and spidery arms and legs, except that her hair was iron-gray and her skin pure leather and she chain-smoked Camel Lites. By now, Peggy would have her clubs stowed in her shiny red golf bag, the same bag she had used in her golfing triumphs forty years ago—women's champion seven years straight at the Carthage Country Club, multiple championships in Raleigh, Pinehurst, and Wilmington. She would have lugged the bag out to the curb in front of her condominium and would be sitting on the grass, cross-legged, smoking, having forgotten nothing, extra balls, kidskin gloves, flask of gin.

Carolyn removed her robe and gown and headed into the bathroom to shower. As she passed a window, she saw Alan walking around a clear space near the azalea hedge where he had coaxed some Bermuda grass to grow last year. He was taking long even strides and she realized he must be pacing off the area where the gazebo could go. Gazing out the window she suddenly saw it, a gracefully rounded white structure with a peaked green roof, latticed railings, steps on two sides, not a

cage at all but a miniature theater. "You and Mr. M can sit out
there in the ev'nin' and drink your cocktails," Alan had said last
summer. She hadn't had the heart to tell him she and John never had cocktails together anymore—if John did get home for
dinner he wanted to eat right away, then watch TV before bed.
But Alan's imagination must have been contagious because
suddenly she saw the two of them, herself and John, seated in
white wicker chairs in the gazebo. She saw John reach over and
take her hand and squeeze it.

"Alan!" she yelled out the window.

He looked around, still pacing.

"Up here, Alan!"

When he saw her at the window, he stopped and stared.

"Alan, I want it! I want the gazebo! Go ahead and start
building it."

He didn't say anything, just stared.

She yelled louder, "I *want* the gazebo, Alan!"

He still didn't say anything, though he flipped his hand in
an assenting gesture. She smiled and waved gaily and stepped
back from the window, feeling wonderful. Then she looked
down at her white naked self and groaned.

She and Peggy were alone on the course. The acres of vel-
vety fairways and scissored greens lay mostly vacant during
the week, at tremendous expense to the club. Weekends were
crowded, though. At one time she had played every Saturday
in a mixed foursome with John and another couple, a custom
long since abandoned. Her game had never been more than
mediocre; today it was atrocious, since all she could think

about was that moment at the window—what Alan had *seen,* what he must *think.*

"Tee it up again, sweetie," Peggy told her when she topped the ball on the first tee, but she doggedly exchanged her driver for a three iron, strode out the thirty feet, and hit a low looping shot that landed on the lip of a pond.

"It's just concentration," Peggy said, after firing a long arching ball straight down the fairway. "It's all in the mind."

As if Carolyn didn't know that. And what was in her mind was what Alan Turner had seen—*all* of her from the waist up. Though it was possible the angle had prevented his getting a good view. She'd check that out when she got home. Meanwhile, she trudged down to the pond to chop her ball out of the weeds.

Her mother-in-law continued in excellent form, parring the first hole and bogeying the second, until they got to the famous number three, "Old Hell Hole." "God a'mighty," Peggy cried as her ball, after a heartbeat of hope, hooked left into the woods and descended with a discreet disturbance of dry branches into the underbrush. Carolyn steered the cart to the edge of the fairway, where her mother-in-law hopped out and plunged into the rough, warning, "Don't come in here, sweetie. This place is a mess of poison ivy. I'm immune." So she sat in the cart and listened to Peggy's furious attacks on scrub oak, stripling dogwood, and matted pine straw, while overhead, doves murmured their soft consolatory cries. At last a ball dribbled onto the grass and Peggy herself emerged to say with a quiver of belief, "All's well that end's well."

By the sixth hole (they customarily played only nine), Peggy was returning from the adventurous places her erratic ball led her—woods, sandpits, creeks—with her leather cheeks stained pink, full of mirth and gin. Where on her small person she hid the flask had always been a mystery.

"Honey, this is not my *day*." Peggy sprang stiffly onto the cart's seat. "You seem a little off your game too. That son of mine hasn't upset you, has he?"

"John's been out of town all week," Carolyn said. "But my yardman came today. You know how that is."

"Lord, yes. I've had a hundred of 'em. You think it's safe to leave him? Did you lock the house?"

"Oh, I don't worry about Alan."

They were gliding up the long hill of number seven and she felt her face getting hot. She could smell the dry sharp grass and feel the slick oily sweat under her arms.

"He's the one who's going to build a gazebo for me," she said.

"You're still going after one of those?" Peggy lit a fresh Camel and exhaled fiercely. "I couldn't take all the mess and racket, but you're younger than I am."

"It'll be fun. Alan and I are going to design it together. I haven't had a chance to mention it to John. He comes home tonight."

"Well, you need a little pleasure in your life, sweetie, and if a gazebo'll give it to you, I'm all for it. You tell my stick-in-the-mud son I said so." Then she hopped out of the cart to slam her ball straight into a pine tree.

When they finished the ninth hole, they parked the cart and went into the clubhouse, where Carolyn decided to join

Peggy in a martini. Frank D., Peggy's special waiter since her glory days, seated them in what was still known as the ladies' bar, a sunny room with white and gold rococo tables and beige banquettes. When he set down Peggy's glass, Beefeater's, extra dry, garlanded with frost, and murmured, "Here you are, Miz Martin," her mother-in-law's gray eyes glowed like Christmas in her wizened child's face, the way they must have glowed back in the Forties when she was Miss Peggy Battle, dancing and golfing all over the eastern part of the state. "A real charmer," Carolyn's father used to say, having danced with Peggy Battle at the debutante parties of '49. Her mother always added elliptically, "What a shame."

"Peggy, I'm only going to have one," she announced firmly as they raised their glasses. "Then I've got to eat my salad and run."

"Sweetie, we're here to relax. We earned it out on that golf course. You know, I don't recognize a damn soul in there."

Her mother-in-law was staring into the large airy Florida room that opened off the ladies' bar, where several dozen colorfully dressed women sat at tables of bridge, chattering like parakeets. The day had been when Peggy could have named every woman in the room, along with her family pedigree, none of which would have been as impressive as her own, the Battles having been the first family of Carthage since the Creation, owning thousands of acres of pine woods, the local bank, and tobacco markets across four states.

"Who's that little girl with the fancy hairdo?" Peggy asked. "Do I know her?"

Carolyn could not place the girl with the fancy hairdo.

Emily something? Husband with the new bank? John would know. She sipped her martini, awaiting the warm tingle she was counting on to calm her down and make her stop seeing herself emblazoned bare-breasted in the window that morning. On the other hand, for all she knew, Alan might be near-sighted.

"Frank D., this martini's mighty near perfect," Peggy rasped in her smoker's alto. "Where are you, Frank D.?"

"Right here, Miz Martin. Are you ready for another one?" Frank D. was a short dapper man, bald, with taffy-colored skin. He had taught social studies at the black high school until integration, when he lost his teaching job and started working at the club. That was thirty years ago.

"Frank D.," Carolyn interrupted, "I'd like to order my chicken salad now. I'm sorry to rush, Peggy. I'm getting nervous about my yardman."

"There's not much out there for him to ruin, if you don't mind my saying so," her mother-in-law said. "Yes, I'll have another, thank you, Frank D."

The waiter hurried off to the bar. Frank D. took care of Miz Martin first; others waited their turn. This had been going on for years, and everyone was used to it, except John. "Mother has no sense of how things look and never has," he often said. John did not appreciate his mother the way Carolyn did. How could he? For years, while Peggy flirted and caroused at parties, trying to keep her belle days alive—she had been famous at one time for dancing on tabletops—he had stood silently beside his father, both men holding themselves as stiff as though they were ironed, waiting for the inevitable moment when they would be called upon to step forward, help Peggy to her feet, nod politely to embarrassed onlookers, and support her to the car. Jack Martin had made it a point of honor never to criticize his wife no matter what she did. In his later years, he rarely spoke to her at all. All this had taken its toll on John. "Mother's like a child. She'll do anything to get attention," he had said once in an uncharacteristic outburst. "Your mother's just having fun," Carolyn had tried to soothe him. Don't you see how *unhappy* your mother is? she had wanted to say, remembering Papa Jack's rigidity, his terrible silences. But John wouldn't have viewed unhappiness as an excuse for bad manners.

He would have been horrified if he knew that Frank D. regularly drove his mother home from the club. Carolyn had forgotten how it started, her saying good-bye after lunch and Peggy remaining ensconced in the ladies' bar, well cared for and happy, until Frank D. got off work at five. He would help her to his elderly Eldorado, a spotless robin's egg blue, and drive her the five miles into Carthage. At Peggy's condo, he would escort her to her door, carrying her golf bag over one shoulder, set the bag inside, perform an old-fashioned bow, and leave. Though Carolyn had never witnessed this scene, others had and had mentioned it condescendingly, though not, fortunately, to John. John would have viewed the arrangement as a scandal.

John was short like both his parents, with his father's stocky, squared-off build. Carolyn had begun dating him when she was in her junior year in college and John in his first year of law school. They married two years later, enabling him to avoid

Vietnam, though that had not been their intent. He had been a polite, serious young man whose brown eyes followed her adoringly as she danced around their kitchen, serving up the harum-scarum meals that used to be her specialty, artichokes with canned crab, tuna in aspic with olives. But with age, John had acquired a brusque, abstracted manner, which she attributed to the pressures he put on himself at work; he was a successful lawyer, traveling often to Washington and Atlanta. When he came home, he seemed not to know quite where he was. She'd tease him, make faces, waggle her fingers at him from behind her ears, and he would smile, but she could see the puzzlement—or was it disappointment?—in his eyes when he looked at her.

"If I were you, I'd let him handle whatever it is," her mother-in-law was saying, apparently still talking about the yardman. "They always know better than you. I had one, his name was Gus, I'd ask him to spray the roses for blackspot and he'd say, 'Not time yet, Miss Peg.' I'd point to the yellow places on the leaves and Gus'd say, 'Not time yet, Miss Peg.' Drove me crazy. Then when I thought I'd lost all my Queen Elizabeths and the floribunda for sure, he'd decide it was time to spray, and he'd spray and spray. The neighbors thought we were fumigating the universe. But the blackspot would disappear and every-thing would be fine and dandy. Do you remember Gus, sweetie, or was he before your time?"

Carolyn smiled. It seemed to her there was no time before she had known Peggy. She could even, almost, imagine telling her mother-in-law what she'd done that morning. *You exposed yourself to the yardman, sweetie? Well, he can consider himself a lucky son of a gun.* Poor "lucky" Alan was probably at this moment still in a state of shock. She giggled.

"You have to laugh," Peggy agreed, "or go bats."

The noise from the Florida room grew louder as the bridge players rose like a flock of startled birds so their tables could be reset for lunch. Several of their number drifted into the bar and called out greetings to the two of them in their corner. A blonde in tomato red linen tripped over to give Peggy a peck on the cheek.

"Miz Martin, how in the world *are* you? Hey there, Carolyn."

"Well, look who's here," Peggy cried, clearly without any idea who the girl was.

"I'm Ashley Wofford, Miz Martin," the blonde said, unfooled. "Kay Davis's daughter. I just had my hair highlighted."

"Tell your mother to call me up, honey. We need a good gossip before all our crowd dies off and there's nobody to talk about."

As other girls flurried around Peggy, the blonde turned and demanded severely, "Carolyn Martin, where have you *been?* I haven't seen you in ages."

Carolyn cocked her head and smiled coyly. Privately she called Ashley Wofford the gusher. Her husband was in John's firm.

"Seriously, Carolyn." Ashley bent over her in a cloud of Faberge. "Some of us were talking about you the other day. We're worried about you stuck out in that big house all by yourself."

"John's there," she said, opening her eyes wide.

"John Martin works like a dog. Everybody knows that. He's never home, now is he? Aren't you scared out there by yourself? I would be."

Even as she rattled on, Ashley's cool eyes drifted to Frank D. leaning on the bar, reading a newspaper.

"If you really want to know, Ashley," she said quietly, "I spend my time running naked around my house."

Ashley's eyelids fluttered. Her lacquered smile stiffened.

"It makes you feel marvelous. Very free. I highly recommend it. I probably wouldn't do it if I still lived in town. Too many prying eyes, you know."

Ashley patted her arm. "You're a trip, Carolyn. But you better watch what you tell people. Somebody's going to take you seriously one of these days."

"Now remind me who your mother is, honey," Peggy was saying loudly to one of the others.

"Come on, girls." Ashley's face was a smooth mask. "We better go eat our shrimp before they shrivel up on us. Bye, Miz Martin. I'm gonna tell Mama to call you. Bye, Carolyn."

"Bye, Ashley," she murmured as they fluttered off. Her face tingled as though she had a rash. What had possessed her, saying such a thing?

"Where's Frank D.?" Peggy demanded. "We need another one after that onslaught."

Warmed by a second martini and fattened by chicken lumps and mayonnaise, Carolyn announced she had to go.

"You run along, sweetie," Peggy rasped through her smoke.

"I'll be *fine*. Frank D. and I have a lot to talk about. We're set-tling our differences on affirmative action."

She leaned closer. "I know that son of mine's told you not to let Frank D. drive me home. But honey, I'm a lot safer with him than with the other old coots who might be dancing at-tendance. Frank D.'s a perfect gentleman, but don't tell Johnny. I want him to worry."

Somewhere in the recesses of the club, rock music played, the kind her son and daughter listened to. Through the music, chirrupy laughter wafted in from the Florida room, where the bridge club was eating shrimp and gossiping. *Carolyn Martin's such a trip,* Ashley Wofford would be saying, which was code for *Carolyn Martin's becoming an eccentric alcoholic like her mother-in-law.*

"Except for you, honey," Peggy was saying, "Frank D.'s the only person I enjoy talking to anymore. His wife died ten years ago, the same year as Jack. He and I have a lot in common. You'd be surprised."

No I wouldn't, she wanted to say. Hadn't Alan broadened her view of the world, too? Alan, who was probably telling Melody at this very moment what he'd seen that morning. Would Melody be angry? shocked? laughing her head off?

"Can I get you anything, Miss Carolyn?"

The waiter's creamy brown face appeared above her, his large intelligent eyes inquiring. Instead of getting up to leave as she had planned, she ordered dessert.

Dreamily she consumed forkfuls of the club's famous choc-olate pecan pie while Peggy and Frank D. carried on an ani-mated conversation about issues in the news she had long since lost track of. As she tasted the heavy sweetness on her tongue, she was aware again of her body surrounding her like a soft cocoon. *She's gotten big as a house. Do you think it's glandular?* Her glance drifted toward the Florida room, from which a fierce Amazonian chattering now emanated. She imagined the girls staring out at their threesome in the bar, the tiny old woman in her aura of cigarette smoke, the large, fair younger one stuffing herself, and the black waiter who had drawn up a chair and was volubly conversing, a breach of club etiquette to be tolerated only because of Peggy Battle Martin's special status in the community, itself almost a thing of the past as new people moved in who did not know about family lineage, or care.

"I'm all for black people going to college," Peggy was declaring. "I just think they ought to pass the same exams as everybody else to get in."

"Peggy," Frank D. replied in his warm reasonable voice, "you know as well as I do blacks are just as smart as whites, but a lot of them still can't pass those tests. Now what are we going to do about *that*?"

He calls her Peggy, Carolyn thought.

"The youngsters have got to study harder," Peggy continued. "You ought to go back and teach them yourself, Frank. You know more history than anybody I ever heard of."

"Why I'm as old as you. We *are* history, Peggy. Who's going to listen to us?"

Peggy chuckled and picked up the coffeepot. Frank D. held out his cup and she poured. Carolyn blinked. A whole new scenario began to unroll. How strange life was if you opened your eyes.

"Honey, are you still here?" Peggy cried as Carolyn rose from her chair.

"I'm leaving now, Peggy. No, don't get up, Frank D."

She reached down and enfolded her mother-in-law in her arms, careful not to crush the fragile bones. What on earth would she do without Peggy?

"That son of mine leaves you alone too much," Peggy murmured into her shoulder. "I could kill him."

"John does his best, Peggy," Carolyn said, tenderly. "He does what he can."

The pink gateposts poked up among scrub oak and bracken on the Carthage road, two phallic spires with fake Roman swags and brass letters spelling out "Wilde Woode Estates" and, underneath, "Private." They never failed to make her wince. What did strangers think as they drove past? Did they try to imagine the sort of person who lived inside those gates? If it were she, she might turn in to see for herself, but as far as she knew no passerby ever had. All a motorist would glimpse, of course, would be pretentious houses, like the massive Tudor just inside the gate, and beyond that, a creamy Tara with miniature pillars, and next, a bright yellow Italian villa—no *people* anywhere, unless it was a large middle-aged white woman walking alone on the shoulder of the road, as she sometimes did in the late afternoon.

As the lake glittered ahead, she turned in at their house, a two-story red brick American colonial. The driveway was empty, the blue truck gone. She pulled her car into the garage and turned off the motor. Alan had left, probably for good, out of fear of what she might do next. Their gazebo would die a natural death. She was relieved, or ought to be, she told herself as she walked slowly into the house.

But no. On her kitchen table under the sugar bowl, she found a note: "Finished seeding. DON'T WALK NEAR FINCE. Back tomorrer with lumber," signed with a flourish, "ALAN." Her heart pumped with timid gladness. He had not abandoned her after all. No word about the incident. Well, of course not. What would he say? *The sun was in my eyes when you showed your nekkid breasts out the window.* Or, *Don't worry, Miz Martin, you look real good for your age.*

He had also left a new drawing. The roof decoration had been eliminated and the gazebo looked square and clunky, more like a hot dog stand than a summerhouse, not at all her airy vision of the morning. She frowned, imagining John's reaction. *A toolshed perchance?* She moved to the stove to put water on for tea, feeling the soft heaviness of her body and imagining the disappointment in John's eyes as he looked at her. Life had not been what he had expected either.

It's a gazebo, John. I plan to paint it white and grow wisteria over it and a zillion petunias around it.

Ah. Are you thinking of becoming a landscape designer? There's good money in that, I hear.

The yardman designed it. It's for us.

I see. You're spending money then, not making it.

Oh, John! I'm trying to make things different for us. Don't you see? John, look at me!

She made tea in her old Chi Omega mug and carried it out onto the darkening lawn. The western sky showed streaks of vivid pink and orange. They didn't see sunsets in town, John had told her when he was pointing out the advantages of the new house, though she couldn't remember his viewing a single one since they'd moved out here. Speaking of viewing, she thought, and looked up at her window. The window was dark; it was impossible to tell how much of her Alan might have seen. *An eyeful, honey,* Peggy's voice whispered. *He got an eyeful.*

She sat down on the scrubby grass, set the mug beside her, and stretched out her large white legs. Bending over, she eased off her golf shoes and ankle socks. The cool grass prickled her toes. She smiled. *An eyeful.* Well, why not? In one swift movement, she pulled her shirt off over her head. Arching her back she reached around, unhooked her bra, and tossed it aside, gasping at the shock of cool air on her breasts. She struggled to her feet, unbuttoned her skirt and let it slide to the ground. Then she removed her underpants. She gave a little twirl, feeling parts of her jiggle unfamiliarly, but the feeling didn't bother her—she liked it. Holding out her arms for balance, she began to dance. Amazingly, the steps of the English country dance from her long-ago girlhood came back to her exactly as she had performed it as Queen of the May, step-step-dip twirl, step-step-dip—

Out on the road, a white Cadillac turned in at the pink gates and glided noiselessly past the enormous houses that were nearly invisible in the gathering dusk. The car slowed, pulled into the driveway, and stopped; a man got out, a short, thick man whose head bowed as he pulled a briefcase out of the car and walked to the house. On the lawn she heard nothing, not the car, not the front door, not even the *click* as the back door opened and closed. Lost in the delight of the recovered dance, she dipped and twirled, her pale body moving in gentle madrigals across the patchy grass, step-step-dip, turn-step-dip— She lifted her arms and her breasts swayed heavy and free. She stretched out her leg and looked down at the wide, white, flowing flesh and smiled. She stood on her toes and twirled, feeling her whiteness flame like a candle in the fading light.

From the shadows near the house, a solitary pair of hands began to clap. She faltered for a moment but did not stop. Nor did the clapping; it went steadily on, accompanying her as she dipped and turned. John was looking at her at last. She redoubled her efforts, twirling and dipping, dipping and twirling. She had no idea what would happen after the dance was over—what would he say? what would *she*? Dip-dip-dip twirl! Turn-turn dip! She let that thought go as she went on turning and weaving across the lawn, dancing only for him whose clapping hands echoed the beating in her bare and hopeful breast.

Carpe Diem

❧

The "shadow line," Kurt calls it. Carroll believes he is referring to age, to some transitional moment into old age. But what moment exactly? When we are too old to make love? Too tired to feel desire? Kurt shrugs. When our hopes are extinguished? When I'll never see you again? What line are you talking about, Kurt?

Kurt is almost fifty but looks younger. His hair is a dark silky brown. His skin is smooth. There is a youthful leprechaun quality about him, though he is beginning to have a paunch about the belly. He does not get enough exercise. If he could ski regularly, he says, he would lose that flab. Kurt is an expert skier. He learned to ski when he was five, in Germany. When he was eleven, he had a terrible accident that broke both legs below the knee. The fractured fibulas erupted through flesh and skin. Carroll, drawing her finger along the deep scars on Kurt's calves, tries to envision the accident, the broken skis, the bloodied snow, the boy lying there in the snow, waiting for someone to come.

But she has a hard time picturing Kurt as a boy. Sometimes she has a hard time remembering what he looks like now. Though they have been together for nearly two years, loosely speaking—she has her own place, he has his—they really do not see that much of each other. Kurt is a free-lance photographer and is often traveling. Benin. Djibouti. Sucre. Carroll, too, is busy. She owns and runs a nursery school called Sunshine Day for three- and four-year-olds. Sometimes months go by when Carroll and Kurt do not see each other, though sometimes, out of the blue, he will call from some distant place. She will hear his voice, high-pitched and tentative, as if he did not expect her to answer (or perhaps it's the connection that makes it sound that way?)—*Hello? Remember me?*—and she feels such happiness it terrifies her. Does he actually believe she has forgotten him?

And yet, in certain ways, she does forget. Today, standing in her school yard among all the small revved-up bodies and high, yelling voices, sniffing the odors of sand and lilac, she tries to conjure his face. She knows his eyes are green, his nose small and sharp, his skin lightly freckled. But she cannot visualize his mouth or the curve of his cheek or his expression when he looks at her. She cannot remember his voice. She expects to hear that voice, though, perhaps in a few hours. Kurt is due back today from Mali. Or is it Niger? The prospect of seeing him makes her giddy. He has been away nearly two months. Even so, even in the midst of her excitement, she can't help asking herself where this relationship is going. The question occurs to her all the time, but whenever she alludes to the future—an offhand reference to season tickets for the opera or a time-share deal on a beach house—Kurt shakes his head.

"Carpe diem," he says, in his lightly accented speech.

And Carroll, though she is not seeking permanence, though she does not believe that relationships require official bonds, though she is happy living on her own and seeing Kurt for compressed periods of passion and good talk, is enraged.

Carpe diem indeed.

"Are you all right? You don't look so good," says Judy, Carroll's energetic assistant at Sunshine Day.

"I have a headache," Carroll lies. Or perhaps she does have a headache. A little one.

Judy nods sympathetically. She is twenty years younger than Carroll—out of college only a year—and relentlessly cheerful.

"So what's on the program today?" Judy asks, though she surely knows. It is spring and they are celebrating small animals, rather than Easter, as schools did when Carroll was a child. This being Washington, D.C., nearly half the children are from other countries, Vietnam, France, El Salvador, the Sudan, some of which do not celebrate Easter.

"Rabbits," Carroll says. "We're doing paper bunnies today. I've still got to cut them out."

"By the way," Judy steps closer. "Guess who dropped Paul off today."

"His father," Carroll says sarcastically. Paul's father has never dropped him off.

"His mother," Judy says. "They've lost their babysitter again."

Carroll glances at Paul, a curly-headed blond boy lost in his own world as he balances on the wooden climbing blocks.

She thinks of his mother, a trim brunette who drives a silver Mercedes convertible in which there is scarcely room for Paul because of the large Labrador that always occupies the front seat. The father is much older, heavy and shambling, probably a drinker. Carroll has met him only once, when the parents came to sign Paul up for Sunshine Day.

Bellows of grief interrupt her musing on Paul. It is Julio, the youngest child in the school, a small brown-skinned boy who is always falling down and skinning his knees. Judy sprints toward him and gathers him into her capable arms. Judy is very good with the children. She could easily run Sunshine Day for a few days or a week if Carroll wanted to go away, as she has often imagined doing, accompanying Kurt on one of his trips. Capri. Cape Town. Caracas. Suddenly, she wants him so much her heart hurts. Literally. The burning in her chest makes her think of Julio's scraped knee. She will have to tell Kurt when he calls that she cannot go on with this. Perhaps, she thinks, it has to do with the "shadow line." Maybe she has passed it, whatever it is. Maybe she has lost hope.

Julio's sobs peter out as he nestles in Judy's lap. Carroll walks over to them.

"Will you be okay out here if I go cut out the bunnies?" she asks, knowing Judy will be fine.

Judy smiles up at her. It occurs to Carroll that Judy would probably be ecstatic to be left in charge while Carroll took a trip with Kurt. But would Kurt be happy? That is the question. She truly doesn't know.

Settled on a low stool at one of the art tables, preparing to cut silhouettes of rabbits out of colored paper, Carroll looks fondly around at her classroom, at the water table that can be transformed into a sand table, the block corner filled with a tremendous teetering fort, the art corner furnished with easels and jars of paints and little smocks hanging on hooks. The dress-up corner is heaped with hats, boots, high heels, frilly sequined dresses contributed by various parents and by Carroll herself. Among her contributions is a pink Mexican shawl she bought when she was still married and she and her husband went to Acapulco on vacation. Also a nightgown her husband gave her, a dark, heavy cotton, long-sleeved, high-necked, not at all sexy. Like the marriage, she thinks. But she settled all that long ago. Now here is the new place she has created. Plants bloom on the windowsills, gerbils race around cages filled with vegetables and gerbil toys. It occurs to Carroll that if carpe diem applies to anyone, it is to children in nursery school. She will pass on this insight to Kurt if she sees him tonight.

She begins cutting out a crimson bunny. It bothers her that Judy has noticed her state of mind. It's happened before, when Carroll has been upset about Kurt. She is often tempted to tell Judy about Kurt, but so far, she has resisted. There is no reason for secrecy; it just seems to be what she and he prefer. What really bothers her, she knows, is that she concentrates on Kurt so much. He is in her thoughts all the time, or hovering on the fringes. It is her first experience with obsession and she finds it daunting. Do normal people feel this way? Is she ill?

In the beginning, when she and Kurt first knew each other, Carroll was the more emotionally independent, or so she believed at the time. She had resolved her guilt over her divorce and come to terms with the division of her son Jamie's life between his father's condo in Bethesda and her small stuffy apartment in Adams-Morgan. Single again, she established her school in a church basement and acquired new friends, artists, professors, poets. She sailed into parties solo, a medium-sized brunette, articulate, self-assured, only slightly panicked by the fact that she didn't have a man, that sex was mostly bad, that she was afraid much of the time. Then one night, there was Kurt standing by the refreshment table, diminutive, dour, nonetheless sending out signals of readiness and passion.

"I like this man" was her first thought, revised to "I think I might like this man."

They retreated to a corner, ignoring the other guests, while he told her a long story about crossing the Sahara in a Jeep. A week later they met for dinner, then a museum, a movie—until one evening they ended up in her apartment, making love. At school the morning after, as she stood groggily pinning drawings of Pilgrims and Indians to a bulletin board, she remembered his avid lovemaking and thought, "Yes. I like him."

Then Kurt disappeared somewhere—Aden, Alice Springs, Aix-en-Provence. She didn't see him for months. He sent her a postcard from Dakar and a book of poems by a Senegalese poet, which she read and put on a shelf. She went through a brief unsatisfactory affair, a successful money-raising drive for her school, a difficult period with Jamie. One day, exhausted, she found herself back in Kurt's sturdy arms.

"You were parked in front of my apartment when I came home that day," she likes to remind him. "The hood was up on your car. You were leaning over it. I thought you were a mechanic."

It is always Carroll who initiates these discussions of their mutual past. Kurt is not interested in sentimental reminiscence.

"A problem with the fuel pump," he says, precise as always.

"We went to my apartment and didn't get out of bed for fourteen hours," she persists, overwhelmed by this memory, only slightly exaggerated.

Even Kurt smiles and shakes his head. Both are astonished by their passion (they are not, after all, seventeen), which for two years now has shown no signs of abating. In fact, it is fiercer than ever.

"What are we going to do?" Carroll sometimes asks after they have made love.

She doesn't know what this passionate, unresolved relationship means. Are they friends? lovers? ships in the night?

Kurt answers, though perhaps with less conviction now than before, "Carpe diem."

Carroll's closest relationship, other than with Kurt, is with her son. Jamie lives mostly with his father, not out of preference, though he and his dad get along well, thankfully, but so that he can attend a good public high school. He is supposed to stay with her on weekends, but that rarely happens, certainly not for whole weekends, now that Jamie has his lacrosse, his girlfriend, his driver's license. He comes for Sunday brunch when he doesn't need to sleep late, occasionally to dinner. Carroll has, in fact, told Jamie about Kurt, a little, to assure him she is not entirely friendless—manless is what she thinks he thinks. She has shown Jamie the things Kurt has given her, beaded slippers from Uganda, swaths of silk from Kyrgyzstan, wind pipes from Bolivia. Jamie's young beautiful face remains solemn as he says, "He sounds cool, Ma." She is lucky to have a son like Jamie. One day she will arrange for the three of them to have dinner.

Kurt, too, has a son. He was married when he was very young to a girl from his hometown in Germany. She has seen Max only in pictures—one picture, to be exact; Kurt, the photographer, does not believe in photographing people he knows. Max is twenty-one and lives in Munich. Kurt sees him three or four times a year, en route from Cairo or Kuala Lumpur or wherever he happens to be working. But he rarely talks about Max. Kurt has told her they should keep their personal lives separate. In a way, this seems unnatural to her; in another way, she agrees. When they are together, everything else is irrelevant.

The last time Kurt was home, he stayed for nearly four months, long enough for her to get used to seeing him regularly. They spent evenings at her place, talking, drinking wine, listening to music, making love. Carroll's apartment is furnished with afghans and hassocks, bookcases made of planks propped on cinder blocks, lots of plants. It resembles the apartment she had years ago when she was a graduate student. When she looks at it, she sometimes thinks she is trying to go back to that time before marriage, trying to start again.

Kurt appears to enjoy her apartment. He stretches out on the tatami and tells her about the countries he has visited, the people he has met. She pictures him hurtling along the top of the Andes in his Citroën, wading through tide pools in New Guinea, climbing Mayan pyramids in Palenque, his cameras dangling dangerously from one shoulder, his eyes narrowed and his lower lip protruding defiantly as he concentrates on avoiding the many hazards of his life. A single misstep and he is gone. Sometimes he has that expression when he looks at her.

By and large, she believes him when he says he does not involve himself with women on his travels, that he works too hard and the risk is too great. Anyway, there is something virginal about Kurt. Or damaged. Kurt is a man who is extremely, excessively, wary of women. Carroll wonders about his German childhood, so different from her own American one. He has told her bits and pieces about his cold fanatical mother, his absent father, his wife who left him. Are these why he has such trouble expressing his feelings? Why he avoids commitment? Why he has never told Carroll he loves her? Then why is she, in contrast, uncharacteristically verbal? Is it perhaps in response to his reticence? "I like this with you so much," she is always saying, picking up a little of his accent, and sometimes, not always, he replies, "Well, so do I like it or I wouldn't be here." A remark that both reassures and irritates her.

Maybe, she thinks, it is a problem of language. English is after all his third or fourth. The last time they were together, before he left for wherever he is returning from now, she told him about a new child at Sunshine Day, a little Basque boy named Didier who speaks almost no English but has become best friends with an American girl named Jennie. She described how Didier and Jennie play together, wordlessly, with perfect equanimity, and Kurt smiled. Perhaps it reminded him, as it does her, in a way, of themselves.

Sometimes, not often, they go to his house to listen to music and look at his artifacts. Kurt is a collector of rocks, stones, beads, masks, native pottery. He has shelves and shelves of these things, some of them quite valuable, all fascinating to Carroll. They go over them together, item by item. Kurt's house is like a museum, beautiful, interesting, and, in Carroll's view, totally impersonal. There are none of those random objects that tend to litter her place—crumpled envelopes with phone numbers scribbled on them, postcards, old ticket stubs; she hates to throw anything away. In Kurt's domain she is always a little uneasy, as though she might break something, or leave a smudge.

But Kurt seems to like to have her there, and she enjoys the spare, white rooms. He gives her wine and spreads a quilt on the floor and puts Bolivian windpipe music on the stereo. This music manages to reach some deep, secret part of Carroll she never knew existed. What is that? she cries at the sound of a high piercing whistle that makes her want to weep and take Kurt into her immediately. Charango, he replies. Then he tells her about a mountain village near La Paz where he once listened to this music as the shadows crept up from the valleys and the sky grew dark. Three men played instruments and a woman sang in a high, high voice and two other women danced. Everyone else, the Indians and Kurt, stood in a circle and listened, totally silent, totally still.

"No one said anything, no one moved. It was like—"

He pauses, searching for words. His English is excellent, but at certain moments, she has noticed, he seems to draw a blank.

Finally, he says, "—like paradise."

And she imagines him on the mountaintop with the wind-pipes and the swaying dancers and the circle of dark silent people. He will surely go back someday, probably without her. But then he leans toward her, kisses her. And she wants him so much she thinks she might pass out.

But is this wanting enough? The question plagues her. Shouldn't they somehow make this thing more? Shouldn't they plan a future? Whenever she mentions this idea, Kurt's face wrinkles like a paper bag. A look of suffering darkens his eyes and he begins talking about Zambia, Bogotá, the Grand Caymans. By the time he left this last time, Carroll was not sure she had the strength to continue whatever it was they were having together. She begins to rehearse a speech she intends to make to Kurt, perhaps that very evening. Listen, she will say, we have to decide what we're doing. Where is this thing going? I have to know. She hears her imagined voice rising shrilly and clips an ear off a lime green bunny.

The children stomp back into the classroom, scrambling into chairs around the tables without being told to. They know art is next. One of the secrets of a successful nursery school, Carroll has discovered, is that there aren't any surprises. The children must always know what will happen and the order it will happen in; story time will be followed by games and games by playground and playground by art. Repetition is the way they acquire a sense of security—which is exactly what she does not have with Kurt. She never knows whether what they do together will ever happen again. Perhaps that is the reason that, whenever he leaves on a trip, she reverts to the child's early view of separation and expects never to see him again.

She walks around, placing large cans of crayons in the center of each table. The children are excited about decorating the bunnies, which Carroll will hang up with clothespins on a string across the room. They get to work immediately. After only a few minutes, a small redheaded girl named Maggie, a Norman Rockwell child complete with braids, freckles, and a lisp, waves her arm for Carroll's attention. Carroll goes over to see what she wants.

Maggie holds up her rabbit for Carroll to admire.

"I like that, Maggie," Carroll says, kneeling down.

She notes that Maggie has decorated her bunny with a mop of bright yellow hair, but she doesn't mention this. She is always careful not to say too much, not to interfere with what the children have on their minds.

"Do you know who my bunny ith?" Maggie whispers.

Carroll thinks she does know. For weeks, Maggie has had a crush on, of all people, Paul. This wild love sometimes happens among children of this age. Carroll respects such feelings.

"It must be Peter Rabbit," she says, innocently.

Maggie shouts with laughter.

"No. It ithn't Peter Rabbit." Maggie cocks her red head on one side and says, slyly, "Ith Paul."

"Oh. Paul Rabbit. Of course!" Carroll stands up and smiles down at Maggie, who is now coloring the rabbit's—Paul's—face a bright orange.

In a little more than two hours, the children will leave. Judy has agreed to perform the cleanup today so that Carroll can make a mythical doctor's appointment. In fact, she will rush home to get out of these stained clothes and wash her hair and wait for Kurt. There is wine in the refrigerator and cheese and she will stop by the market for the Italian bread they both like. She never cooks for him; cooking would imply something neither of them wants to get into yet, though perhaps for different reasons.

But what if Kurt doesn't come back today? Or suppose he does but decides to spend the evening elsewhere? Oh, she can't bear this. She is too old for all this uncertainty, for these terrible adolescent longings.

"Why don't you go on home," Judy says, soothingly, at her elbow. "I'll handle the pickup. No problem."

"Maybe I will," Carroll agrees. But now she is angry. Angry at herself, angry even more at Kurt. It strikes her that he is incapable of carrying on a relationship with a woman who loves him. Why hasn't she seen this before?

If he does call today—she pictures the phone on the table beside her bed, squat and silent as a Buddha—she will tell him exactly how she feels, why it's no longer a good idea for her to see him. She imagines the ringing of the phone. "It's me," he will say, sounding gleeful, like a boy, as he always does when he returns from a trip. Imagining this makes her long to see him, to feel him against her, to smell his skin. Of course she will tell him to come over, right away, that instant. Later, there will be time to tell him how she feels.

Several children are frantically trying to get her attention. They have finished their bunnies and want her to pin them up on the clothesline. Andy Goldsmith has done a slapdash job as usual, which she praises nevertheless. A little girl named Simone, the daughter of a French father and Vietnamese mother, hands over her rabbit, carefully if sparely decorated.

Carroll is busy now, pinning up rabbits, commenting on each one as it is handed to her. Somora Abbai, from the Sudan, holds up her rabbit for Carroll to see, though it is not finished yet. The rabbit has intricate designs on its cheeks and the insides of its ears. Somora is preternaturally gifted. Carroll smiles encouragingly, then goes over to help Denise Hawkins, who is not gifted, write "Denise" in large letters across her rabbit's chin.

Fifteen or so rabbits are marching through the air across the classroom when Carroll notices that Maggie and Paul have left the table and are standing side by side at two easels in the art corner. Paul is painting away while Maggie stares at him, her lips parted, her eyes glistening, enraptured. Carroll wants to shake her. You paint, too, Maggie, she wants to cry. Pick up your brush and paint!

She goes over to the art corner, though her policy is not to interfere in these things. Maggie, perhaps aware of her teacher's approach, dips her brush into a jar of fuchsia-colored paint and diddles with it on her paper. Usually a fearless, creative painter, she produces nothing but scribbles. Meanwhile, Paul is making huge ugly interlocking lines in browns and blacks on his paper.

"That's nice, Maggie," Carroll says.

"Look at what Paul ith doing," Maggie responds immediately.

"Paul's is nice too," Carroll says.

Paul ignores them both.

Behind them at the table, Somora lets out a high shriek. Carroll turns in alarm. Danny Casey has marked Somora's bunny with a red slash across its face. Somora is beside herself, crying hysterically. She has worked so hard on her bunny. Danny is also upset at what he has done; his face is fiery red. Probably he has no idea why he marked Somora's rabbit. Carroll starts toward them, but Judy is already there, kneeling between the two children, talking, soothing, expostulating. Carroll decides she will stay for the pickup, after all. She feels fine, actually. Her headache has gone. Her decision to explain to Kurt that she can't go on with this has made her feel wonderful.

At three o'clock, Danny Casey's father arrives. Danny's mother works across town and his father is usually the one to pick him up, though the father presumably works somewhere, too. Carroll isn't sure what the story is with the Caseys. Somora's mother comes next, a fragile beautiful woman—it is hard to believe she once walked for two weeks across a desert, carrying her tiny daughter on her back. Somora runs up and begins telling her mother about Danny's desecration of her rabbit. The mother listens patiently, silently. What weight do such problems have for her, after what she has been through? She always seems calm, endlessly patient. She smiles at her daughter, nods to Carroll. They leave.

One by one, the children are taken away by mothers and babysitters; Mr. Casey is the only father today. Ironically, Maggie and Paul are the last children left, sitting quietly together on two small chairs in the yard near the door. Carroll thinks what a colorless little boy Paul is. What does Maggie see in him?

Then Maggie's mother, a wild redhead in jeans and T-shirt, rushes in, apologizing for being late. She praises Maggie's bunny extravagantly. They go off, Maggie chattering away to her mother. At the gate they pause, turn, and Maggie waves, probably to Paul, though it is Carroll who waves back.

"Who's picking you up today, Paul?" Carroll asks, making her voice light. She doesn't want him to feel bad about being the last one.

"My mother," he mumbles, but of course it will not be his mother. His mother almost never picks him up. A babysitter comes for Paul. Already this year he has had five or six different babysitters; Carroll has lost count. When one of them quits, as has apparently happened today, a large black woman, presumably the housekeeper, comes for Paul. And yes, here she is, sauntering up twenty minutes late.

Carroll says nothing to the woman about her lateness. She does not want to embarrass Paul. She smiles at him and says, "See you tomorrow."

He marches off across the yard, keeping a careful distance behind the woman who came for him. Carroll notices he is carrying his painting of dark, interlocking lines. As she watches him go, she suddenly envisions him in twenty or thirty years, a slim, good-looking blond man, somewhat quiet, definitely attractive, also cold and withholding. The women who will encounter Paul when he is grown, and fall in love with him, will know nothing about his having to wait to be picked up at school, or the lies about his mother, or the uncaring babysitters. But Carroll knows exactly how it will be—these long-range scenarios of the children's lives often flash into her mind. It is as though she is a wizard. Her knowledge appalls her. Why isn't she able to have such foreknowledge of her own life?

It is then she notices a stocky dark-haired man standing beside the gate, looking at her. She is so shocked she gasps. It is the first time Kurt has come to her school. What does it mean? Her heart lurches and he smiles, enjoying her surprise. He doesn't step inside the gate, though; he waits outside. She starts across the yard. In a few seconds, she will be in his arms, but in those seconds she sees, quite clearly, a boy lying in the snow, staring in terror at his own white bone.

The Minaret

❧

"You get some rest, hon," Bunny said. "I'm gonna find that minaret if it kills me."

She began to close the blinds, heavy, wooden, foreign blinds with slits in them shaped like fish. Through them, she glimpsed her goal for the afternoon, the Turkish minaret, a slender, sand-colored spire rising above the jumble of roofs in the old Greek town. Behind her, Miles lay on the bed in his underpants, reading a paperback copy of *The Iliad*.

"Even the Greeks don't go out at this time of day," she heard him murmur.

She jerked the cord so hard the blinds rattled like snakes. "It won't be so hot in the old town. The sun doesn't get down into those little streets."

Miles grunted. "Watch out for the Vespas. I don't want to have to take home a dead wife."

Dead wife. Have to. Still, she knew what he meant about the traffic. Through the half-closed blinds, she looked down on Heroes Square, flat as a pan and empty in the afternoon, but at night a stew of cars and motorcycles, gunning motors, blaring horns, and the *buzz buzz buzz* of those awful little *motos*. Rethymnon, Crete—"Rest-me-none," Miles called it. They should have gone to Myrtle Beach or—strike that!—to Coney Island. Either would have been more pleasant than idyllic Crete, the place Miles had wanted to visit since he was six and read a child's book about Greek heroes. Since then, he'd read maybe a hundred books about those guys. *Odysseus passed by the island, Bun. Theseus liberated it from the Minotaur.* Bunny had loved his telling her about them.

But Miles was no hero. The heat and noise of modern Crete had felled him. He'd hardly left their room since they arrived on the ferry from Athens four days ago, though the room was a virtual sweat lodge. The hotel they'd thought was such a bargain had no air-conditioning. Who would have believed it, in this climate, in this day and time? Not that the other guests, meaty young Swedes and Germans on package tours, seemed to mind. Bunny saw them cavorting on the city beach, topless women, barely clad men, turning ever deeper shades of nutty brown. For two days she'd trudged around Rethymnon trying to find a cool room. None was available. Drained, exhausted, Miles stayed inside, lying on their bed or sitting on the balcony, venturing out only in the evening for dinner. Only three days remained of their week and they hadn't done any of the things they'd planned. They hadn't even visited that fabled ruin, Knossos.

The room's saving grace, if it had one, was its balcony. From it, they watched the commerce in the street below while they sipped Nescafé in the mornings. Bunny waved to the little girl sorting apricots at the grocer's across the street. She observed

the men sitting in the cafe at the corner. Even Miles enjoyed
their view of the slender minaret that rose serenely above the
din and clatter of the city. In the evenings, while they shared a
bottle of the sharp local wine before the Vespa brigade arrived,
the spire glowed in the reflection of the setting sun, like a jewel
waiting to be found.

And now she was going to find it, as soon as she managed
to close these balky blinds. What was *wrong* with them? As she
struggled, she noticed a couple walking across the empty square
below, a boy and a girl, both wearing shorts and those heavy
walking shoes. The girl's shoulders under her skimpy blouse
were burned purple by the sun. Bunny winced looking at them
and *whap!*, the blinds slapped shut. At last. She turned around.
Miles's eyes were closed. His big white chest rose and fell, rose
and fell. "'Bye, hon," she whispered, picked up her pocketbook,
and slipped out of the room.

She got lost right away. None of the streets in the old town
ran in straight lines and she kept losing sight of the minaret.
One minute it hovered ahead of her; the next, it had slipped
around behind. She came upon the yellow-domed Orthodox
church, but this meant she was too far to the left, so she headed
right and ran smack into the sea wall. She couldn't help laughing. What a town! In America—Well, she wouldn't compare
Rethymnon to Durham, North Carolina. She hadn't realized
things would be so different in another part of the world, this
being her first trip abroad. But that was the reason you trav-
eled, wasn't it? To see how different things could be. She went
into a sweets shop and bought one of those pastries that looked

like shredded wheat and ate it outside, standing in the shade of the wall. The minaret floated airily behind some ocher-colored roofs off to the right. She thought of what she'd say to Miles tonight after dinner. *Just follow me, hon. I'll tell you where we're going when we get there.*

They had tried to find the minaret on their third day, when Miles felt up to a foray into the old part of town. It was clearly marked on their map with a #4. Next to it, #5 was "the largest mosque in Rethymnon." They could hardly miss *that,* Miles had remarked with a smirk. But they had. At some point, they'd stumbled onto #3, a sixteenth-century fountain, four bronze lion heads spitting streams of water into a trough. Miles had splashed some water on his face. He was wearing a shirt, white with blue sea horses printed on it, she'd bought him during their stopover in Athens, and he looked very Greek with his dark eyes and black hair that he wore a little too long for her taste, tendrils trailing on his soft white neck. Bunny often wondered what went through other people's minds when they saw the two of them together, Miles so large and dark with his heavy eyes and soft body, she small and wiry, hair a crinkly brown, freckles all over her face. Did people wonder what he saw in her? She'd been thinking about that at the fountain, when Miles barged off again so quickly she'd had to run after him.

After that, they hadn't followed the map, just turned corners at random. Sweat ran down Miles's large face, and his eyes had that dazzled look a deer's had once, trapped in Bunny's headlights. They passed the fountain again, without stopping. Finally, they emerged into an open space in front of a yellow building that turned out to be the police station. The minaret rose loftily behind them. "Fools!" Miles had whispered, his broad face streaming. "That's what we are. Nothing but a couple of fools!" Bunny had wanted to cry when she heard him say that—not for her sake, for his.

When she finished her pastry, she set out again across a tiny square bright with pink oleander, then plunged down a narrow street that led deeper into the old town. The shutters on the houses were closed, and it was eerily quiet, no sound other than the scuffing of her soles on the gritty stones. The street forked, and she heard the *plink plink plink* of dripping water. There was no sign of the minaret, but she knew it must be near. She entered another street of closed-up houses, their occupants inside out of the heat, probably sleeping. She walked slowly, peering into shadowy alleys. From the mouth of one of the alleys, a gray cat stared out at her. On a whim, she turned in. It was cooler in here, the passage so narrow her shoulders brushed the stone walls. She walked faster. The walls curved and there was the minaret.

She almost didn't recognize it at first. The base was built of huge blocks of pocked yellowish stone, more like a fort than the fairylike spire they saw from their balcony. Craning her neck, she saw the first gallery, encased in an iron grille. There was a second gallery above it—the Koran used to be read from both, simultaneously. What a show that must have been. It hadn't happened in years, of course. There were no Turks in Crete. They were all sent back to Turkey in the 1920s, their mosques converted into offices or left to crumble into ruin. The deserted old buildings made Bunny sad. Such a waste. The minaret, at least, was still intact.

She wandered around the curved base until she came to a flat paved area, like a parking lot, simmering with heat. At its edge was a single tree, and in its smidgen of shade, two people reclined, their heads resting on bulky packs: she recognized the couple she had seen crossing Heroes Square. The girl slept the way a child does, curled in a ball, while the boy sprawled on his back beside her.

She was turning to go when the boy sat up. *Kale spera,* he said, speaking Greek with a heavy American accent.

"Oh, hi," she said. "Are you Americans?"

He nodded. She gave an unnecessary laugh. "Well, you're the first ones we've run into in Rethymnon."

"Who's we?"

What a question. The boy's face was grizzled with a light beard. A ring glinted in one ear. Perhaps he wasn't quite as young as she had first thought.

"My husband and I. We've been here almost a week and, would you believe, this is the first time I've been able to find the minaret."

The boy glanced up at the spire, then back at Bunny. They both looked down at the motionless girl.

"Is she okay?" Bunny asked.

He shrugged. "Wiped out from the heat. We can't find a place to crash."

"Oh, I'm sorry." She felt a pinprick of alarm. "Well, it's nice meeting you. I've got to run."

"Where you off to?"

"Back to the room. I've been exploring while the streets

aren't so crowded. As my husband says, nobody with any sense comes out at this time of day."

"Your husband said that?"

"Well, something like that."

Flustered, Bunny glanced at the ugly yellow stones of the minaret. She wanted to leave, but now the girl rolled over. Her round eyes, glassy as a cat's, peered at Bunny through strings of straw-color hair.

"Lisa, baby, you're alive." The boy touched her shoulder and she shuddered. "This is Lisa. I'm Keith."

They both looked at Bunny. Poor things, Bunny thought in a rush of feeling. They were probably homesick, certainly they were hot and dirty, and they were Americans after all. How could she not do the generous thing?

"Can you believe there's not a room to be had in all of Rethymnon?" she demanded before Miles could speak.

Dressed in a fresh white shirt and slacks, he was sitting at the table reading a day-old copy of the *Herald Tribune*. He looked at her without expression, then at Lisa and Keith looming behind her, huge with their backpacks and clunky shoes.

"Company," he said. "How nice."

"Meet Keith and Lisa." She waved her hand at her exhibits. "They're from California. Sacramento, isn't that right? Students," she added, as though this explained something. "I told them they could take a shower."

"Well," Miles said, "they won't find the facilities exactly what they're used—"

"We're *used*," Lisa interrupted, "to just about anything."

She pushed past Bunny and plopped down on a chair. Just as abruptly, Miles stood up and walked out onto the balcony.

Keith murmured, "Your old man's not too happy about this."

"He'll be fine," Bunny assured him. "Would anybody like a beer?"

Keith shrugged, and she got two bottles of beer out of the small refrigerator. She handed one to Lisa and the other to Keith, who had settled on the sofa.

The cold drink seemed to revive the girl. "Wanna know where we've been?" she asked. She began describing their summer's itinerary: France, Italy, Bulgaria, Greece. Her voice was high-pitched and nasal, surely more New York than California.

Bunny nodded, though her mind was on Miles. She should have thought before she invited these young people. She never did. All those campus strays she invited to dinner back in Durham, homesick freshmen, sad little outcasts. He'd never protested, but this was different. They were in a whole other country.

"We want to go to Sicily now," Lisa said.

"Sardinia," Keith corrected her.

"Wherever." Lisa waved her hand. "I'll be glad to get out of Greece. They're awful to women here. Have you noticed that?"

"Why, no—" Bunny said.

"An old man almost raped me up in the mountains."

She rattled on, explaining how they'd hiked to a remote spot in the mountains, really fabulous but totally nowhere, and while Keith was peeing in the bushes, an old man had appeared and jumped all over her.

"Really?" Bunny was skeptical. "Greeks seem so cultivated, even the poorer ones. They're not a peasant culture, you know."

"Well, they're horny as hell," Lisa said and giggled.

"I'm not at all surprised." Miles's voice floated in from the balcony.

"What do you mean?" Bunny called back. "We haven't seen—"

He was there in the doorway, leaning against the doorjamb. "There's a streak of hardness in these people. Of cruelty. And they've never thought much of women. Read Kazantzakis."

"Oh, I don't agree." Bunny was bewildered. He'd never said anything like this before. But Miles wasn't listening to her. He was looking at Lisa, who had hooked her feet around the legs of the chair. Her bare knees were splayed and her flat chest showed through her skimpy blouse. What an unattractive girl, Bunny thought.

"All I know," Lisa was saying, "is that a dirty old man came up to me and began touching my tits. I was afraid to yell or anything."

"Of course you were," Miles said with a small smile.

"Hey. It was way up in the mountains. Nobody there but goats."

"Zeus's birthplace," Miles said. "Maybe the old man was Zeus."

"Did he actually—?" Bunny began.

"Keith came back then. The old man still had his hands all over me. Keith told him to get lost and he blabbed something and pulled some weeds out of his pocket. He wanted us to *buy* them. Keith gave him some Euros and he gave us the weeds and we left."

Keith had said nothing during this recital. Slumped on his spine on the sofa, he drank his beer and listened, or didn't listen, detached in either case, his long, brown, sinewy legs crossed delicately at the ankles.

Miles sat down at the table opposite Lisa. Bunny brought him a beer and another for Keith. Lisa was talking about a beach on the southern coast, where they had spent the week. They'd wanted to sleep in the caves, she said. There were fabulous caves on the southern coast, but the authorities cleared them every night before dark.

"Can you imagine waking up in one of those caves and looking out and seeing all that water?" Lisa sighed. She was winding a string of hair around one dirty finger.

"If you sleep here," Miles said, "you can wake up and look out on twenty Mercedes, forty Vespas, and fourteen tour buses. Now do you want a shower or not?"

"I think," Miles said, "we should take them to see Knossos tomorrow."

He and Bunny were sitting on the balcony drinking the last of the Tanqueray they had bought at the duty-free shop in New York. It was a little after nine, not quite dark. Traffic swirled around the statue of the Unknown Hero in the square below.

Keith and Lisa napped inside. Bunny had just finished saying, "We'll ask them to leave tomorrow."

"Knossos?" she said now. "Miles, they aren't interested in that kind of thing. Why should we take them?"

At the same time, she was glad Miles was thinking about going to Knossos. He'd read dozens of books about the ancient Minoan palace, its art, its mysterious destruction, sharing his knowledge with Bunny in long dinner-table monologues last winter. She had been preoccupied with practical matters like hotel reservations and the price of airplane tickets and hadn't listened closely. Finally, he'd given up and bought her a copy of *The Bull from the Sea.* She had loved the book. She got goose pimples whenever she thought of Theseus and Ariadne and that poor creature the Minotaur, whom she pitied more than any of the human protagonists, though she knew she wasn't supposed to.

"If they don't want to go to Knossos, they don't have to." Miles was gazing out over the mayhem of the square. "I don't propose holding a gun to their heads."

"Well, we can suggest it. But how long will we let them stay with us? They'll expect us to feed them, you know."

"Lord, Bun. Food here costs practically nothing."

He was right. A meal for the two of them in one of the grubby little restaurants on the esplanade came to barely twenty dollars—roast chicken, green beans, that yogurt dish Miles liked.

"We'll take a bus at eight in the morning," he said.

She wondered whether he was drunk. It wasn't Miles's nature to be generous. She was the generous one, the soft touch, the bleeding heart, always thinking of ways to make students feel welcome in their home, sending birthday cards to her favorites for years after they'd graduated. She believed good deeds had a way of being passed on by those who benefited from them: "pay it forward" was the way she'd heard the idea described. She would never have confided this theory to Miles. His mouth would curl. *That's my Bun. Rings on her fingers and bells on her toes, she will have music wherever she goes.*

At that moment, a herd of Vespas roared into the square. "Ah, the sons of heroes!" Miles shouted, jumping up and raising his glass to the motorcyclists. "Hail, sons of Odysseus!" His voice was so loud people in the street looked up. Embarrassed, Bunny waggled her fingers and smiled at them. At the same time, she was aware of voices in the room. She turned and saw Keith bending over Lisa, rubbing cream onto her burned back. His solicitousness made her ashamed of wanting to get rid of them. What was wrong with her? It might be fun to take the young couple on an outing, like a family.

At dinner, at one of the outdoor eateries that lined the beach, an Australian with a wispy beard came by, crooning ballads. They'd seen him before; it was Miles who'd figured out the man was Australian—something about his vowel sounds. He stood near their table while he sang. Lisa clapped loudly when he finished. The minstrel offered his hat, but Miles ignored it. The man bowed and moved on.

"Do you know anyone in Rethymnon?" Bunny asked.

Had she imagined it, or was there a current of recognition between Keith and Lisa and the singer?

"No way," Keith said. "We just pulled into this burg."

"We've kind of run out of money," Lisa added, her gray eyes as guileless as the sea.

"How unfortunate," Miles said.

There was a silence. Then Bunny said, "Well! I'm glad I found you. It'll be fun for us to have company on our adventure tomorrow."

They'd accepted Miles's invitation to go to Knossos, though Bunny was not at all sure they knew what Knossos was. Keith had simply smiled and said slowly, as though he were spelling the word, "K-nos-sos. Sure. Love to."

"So what's this place you're taking us to?" Lisa asked, looking at Miles.

"Just one of the most important archaeological sites of the ancient world, my dear." Miles's lip curled.

"And now a bunch of rocks, I guess," the girl said.

"Oh my, no. They've restored the palace according to archaeological fact, or fancy, depending on your point of view, complete with wall paintings and red columns, even toilets. Knossos had the earliest known plumbing in the western world, you may be interested to know."

Lisa rolled her cat's eyes. "What about the bull? Have they restored him, too?"

"Ah, the Minotaur. You know something about mythology, do you? I'm impressed."

Lisa playfully stuck out her tongue at Miles, who, to Bunny's surprise, took no notice. He began to describe the palace, its labyrinth of rooms which was probably the basis in history for the mythical maze where the Athenian youth were trapped as food for the Minotaur. Mythical? This was news to Bunny. Was

Theseus mythical, too? She'd thought—Well, never mind what she'd thought.

Miles went on to explain the meaning of various signs that appeared throughout the palace, bull's horns and double axes. As he talked, his large head thrown back, one hand raised, he looked like the teacher he would have been if he hadn't given up history grad school to study library science. They'd been married a year and she'd been too preoccupied with their new life together, the small house they'd bought and thoughts of the children to come, to argue with his decision. If she'd been paying attention, she might have convinced him that he *was* good enough to become a first-rate historian, he *could* stand up to the competition. But she'd gone on her merry way and let him make the mistake of his life, which was why she tried so hard to make it up to him now, why she brought the children home, the freshmen, the strays. Nearly every Sunday they had two or three extras at dinner. "Bunny's little miracles," Miles called them.

When she tuned back in, he was explaining the unknown cataclysm—tidal wave? invasion?—that had destroyed Knossos and the whole Minoan civilization. Keith sat perfectly still, staring at Miles, apparently mesmerized. Lisa was less attentive. Her gray eyes were jumping around in a funny way. "Gotta pee," she whispered to Bunny and pushed back her chair and went into the restaurant.

They ordered coffee. Miles was telling Keith about the attempts, all unsuccessful, to decipher the Minoan language. Keith still seemed interested, though he had stopped asking questions. Lisa had not returned. "Excuse me," Bunny said and got up. She'd never been inside the restaurant. She wouldn't have dreamed of going to the bathroom there.

The girl was standing near a tank of fish, one leg twined around the other, talking to the Australian singer. Bunny stopped by the door. Lisa saw her and waved. She said something to the man, then sauntered over, walking slowly with a swaying motion. Her long legs and neck made Bunny think of a giraffe.

"Want to use the loo?" Lisa said. "I'll show you."

"No thanks," Bunny said. "I was worried about you. I see you've made a friend."

Lisa flipped her hand dismissively at the minstrel, who was crouching down by the fish tank, his mouth moving. Bunny imagined him talking to the fish: *I want to eat you, mate.* Without meaning to, she giggled. Lisa grinned and linked her arm through Bunny's like a conspirator and they returned to the table.

After Miles paid the bill, the four of them walked over to the *fortezza* and stood by the wall, looking out at the sea.

"The wine dark sea," Miles said. "This is it, you know, the very one."

"Wine. Dark. Sea," Keith repeated slowly. "Hey, you a writer or something?"

"Far from it. Though I did once think I might be a writer. One of those youthful flights of fancy. I wonder, do youths still have flights of fancy?"

Without waiting for an answer, he went on, "As it happens, I do deal with books in my profession."

"You sell 'em?" Keith asked.

"I lend 'em. I'm a librarian."

"Where's that?"

"At a small college in North Carolina. My wife works there too, in the development office. She develops."

Bunny smiled self-consciously, though no one was looking at her.

Lisa asked, "Is that where you two met?"

"Oh dear," Miles said. "I don't think we want to get into *that* while sitting on the parapet of one of Crete's fabled hundred cities, to quote the poet."

"We met when we were undergraduates at the state university," Bunny answered anyway. "We got married the summer we got our degrees. Eighteen years ago last June."

"Hey. Congrats," Keith said. "Eighteen years. That'd be a record in my family. Any kids?"

"No," Bunny said. She refrained from saying how much they'd wanted children, how disappointed they were none had come. She'd promised Miles never to say such things in public again, though "no" sounded so forlorn in answer to that question, so insufficient. Just then, the moonlight touched the ring in Keith's ear and it glowed like an ember. She couldn't see his face in the dark, but she was sure he was smiling at her. Again, the bright ember gleamed. It must be the moonlight. Bunny turned and there, so close it seemed she might touch it, was the minaret.

"Oh—"

The others turned and looked, too.

"Miles, we're going to climb that thing tomorrow. I mean it. All the way to the second porch."

"Gallery," he corrected. "And tomorrow we're all going to Knossos."

The bus to Heraklion followed the coast on a curving road that was separated by a border of crimson oleander from a straight drop to the sea. The water below was so dazzlingly blue Bunny's eyes hurt to look at it even through her sunglasses. On the other side, the mountains rose disturbingly close, tall, purplish, emitting the harsh odor of thyme. Miles, sitting by the window, stared out without speaking. He had gotten up before the alarm clock rang and made Nescafé for all of them. They had drunk it on the balcony in the warm blue dawn when the town was perfectly still. Even Lisa, yawning through wispy strands of hair, seemed to share a sense of anticipation.

It was noon by the time they reached Knossos. Miles was sweating heavily, the muscles in his face twitching with nerves. As they bought their tickets and passed through the entry gate, he seemed to be having trouble breathing.

"Are you okay, hon?" Bunny whispered, catching hold of his arm, but he threw off her hand.

"Please *don't.*"

"*Kale spera.*" A tall erect man with a thick black moustache approached. "I can tell you the history of the Palace of King Minos, everything—"

"And charge us a fortune for it," Miles said. "No thank you."

He walked off, followed, after a moment, by Keith.

The guide wore a black crocheted scarf wound around his forehead in the old Greek style. Bunny admired the way he retained his dignity in the face of Miles's rudeness, gazing impassively out of large dark eyes.

"Toilet?" Lisa said to the guide. "Can you—?"

"Come."

"Wait!" Bunny stepped between the man and the girl, but Lisa slipped past her.

"I have to pee real bad. You go on. I'll find you."

The girl was wearing a T-shirt and a long filmy skirt through which her legs were visible up to her crotch. She looked so slatternly with her sloping red shoulders and long lank hair that Bunny felt ashamed. She wanted to tell her to stand up straight and for goodness sakes, keep her legs together. "We'll go slowly," she called. "You can catch up." But Lisa did not look around.

Bunny crossed the courtyard, hot as an oven, and followed a group of tourists through an opening in the wall where, presumably, Miles and Keith had also entered, though she saw no sign of them. The tourists were muscular, dark-haired people, both men and women wearing walking shorts and boots. Their guide, a young Greek woman in a western-style dress, was speaking to them in their language, whatever it was, and Bunny pretended to listen, stopping when the group stopped to inspect a piece of wall, a lump of rock, an enormous jar. They were in a restored part of the palace where paintings had been reproduced on the walls, a colorful procession of dark-haired, wasp-waisted young men holding cups aloft. Bunny admired them along with her adopted companions. *Ja, ja, fery fine,* she murmured. It was something Miles might have said in one of his antic moods. He could be funny when he wanted to be. Oh, where was he?

Eventually, she spotted Keith sitting cross-legged on a terrace several levels below the central courtyard. Miles stood a few feet away, gesturing at a wall, explaining something. "Hi! I'm up here!" she shouted. Miles looked up, scowling. The Greek guide, too, paused in her lecture. Bunny gave her a guilty smile and scuttled off down a staircase. When she reached them, Miles was tapping his guidebook against his leg.

"I hope you weren't—" she began.

"Where's our flower child?"

"She went to the restroom."

Keith shrugged. "Lisa's bladder's a pain to travel with."

Bunny hesitated. She knew how eager Miles was to continue their exploration of the palace, his one chance to pass on his knowledge to someone who might appreciate it. She decided not to insist they wait.

They spent three hours inspecting the palace, much of the time in the unrestored area, scrambling over heaps of stones Miles somehow knew to have been a storeroom or the king's receiving room or the place where the famous bull dance was held. Some of the rocks, he told them, were blackened in the inferno that destroyed the palace nearly four thousand years ago. "Wow," Keith said, widening his eyes. "Long time ago, huh, Bunny?" Bunny tried not to think of Lisa, of where she might be, what she might be doing. She was also worried about Miles. Sweat poured from his face and the sea horses on his shirt clung to his chest, as wet as though they'd been swimming.

At last they collapsed in the shade of a cypress tree. "Hey, man," Keith said, "that was great. How much do you charge?" Miles laughed, his big face glowing, pleased as a child. Bunny hated to spoil the moment by mentioning Lisa. It was Miles who said, "I suppose we should look for our lost lady now."

They found her in the parking lot. She was sitting on a low wall, clutching a bunch of ragged blue wildflowers and a paper cup. "Ouzo," Miles said, sniffing the cup Keith pried out of her hands. Apparently, she had never gone into the palace at all. Giggling, she presented the flowers to Bunny, who stifled an impulse to fling them on the ground and trample them. Keith and Miles each took one of the girl's arms and walked with her to the bus stop. Bunny trailed behind. Several noisy groups of young people were gathered under the acacias. Possibly they had given Lisa the wine. Who knew what had happened? Not that Bunny cared. She simply wanted to go home—wherever home was.

Hours later, after the return bus ride and dinner on the esplanade, during which Miles gave a long discourse on the feminine in Minoan religion to which no one listened, not even Bunny, they were back in the room. Lisa lay down on the sofa without a word and curled into a ball. Keith spread his sleeping bag on the floor beside her.

"Would you like a pillow?" Bunny asked him.

He accepted one with a little bow, then lay down on his back, looking up at her, his opaque blue eyes very wide.

"K-nos-sos," he said slowly. "Wish I'd lived back in those days."

"You do?" She couldn't help sounding surprised.

"Oh sure. Dancing with the bulls. I'd have gone for that. I'd have jumped over those bulls like a real cowboy. The queen and

her maidens in those long skirts, all naked on top, like the little
statue in the museum. Man, that'd be the life."

She stiffened. "It was the priestess who went topless, wasn't
it? I think that's what Miles said."

Keith grinned. "You kill me, Bunny. You and your old man
both kill me."

She had no idea what he meant. She glanced toward the balcony, where Miles sat leafing through the brochures they had
picked up at the museum. Her old man. The back of his neck
was red from the day in the sun. She looked down at Keith. His
arms were folded under his head, his blue eyes fixed upon her
the way they'd been when she first saw him at the minaret.

He said so softly she could hardly hear him, "The world's
real ugly now, Bunny. The crap that goes on—it's vicious out
there."

What was he talking about? She started to tell him the ancient Greeks weren't all kings and heroes, but she was too tired
to get into a philosophical discussion.

Keith gazed at her. "Can I tell you something?"

She nodded.

"I just want you to know you're about the nicest lady I ever
met. That's all. I wish you and your husband the best. I really
do."

Then he closed his eyes. She started to say thank you, but
something held her back. She didn't even say good night. She
turned and walked out on the balcony.

Miles was in an excellent mood. As soon as she sat down, he
began recounting the parts of the day he'd particularly enjoyed.
Seeing the queen's chamber pot. Walking on the fire-blackened

rocks, one of which he'd purloined, by the way. Wasn't he clever? A small one, of course. He would use it for a paperweight at home. Oh, and how did she like the way he'd dodged that guide at the gate?

Bunny remained silent, thinking about what the boy had said—she still thought of him as a boy, though he wasn't one. Closer to thirty than twenty she guessed. Ugly, vicious: what did that mean? And then what he said about her being nice. Did he really mean it? Probably not. Yet she couldn't help but hope. He had remembered a lot of what Miles told him, all that ancient history. Keith might have been a good student, though he didn't seem to have studied much, just as Miles would have been an excellent professor if he'd stuck to it. She would have been a good mother, and Lisa, well, even Lisa might have been different if just one little thing had been altered. Wasn't life funny? She wanted to tell Miles what she was thinking, but just then he yawned loudly. She'd tell him another time.

Later, in bed, conscious of the two on the other side of the room, she whispered, "Sleep well, hon. And thank you for a wonderful day."

She didn't know whether Miles heard her; then he put his hand on her leg. She lay still. He kept his hand there for some time, heavy, warm. Even after he removed it, she felt its weight pressing her skin, reminding her of how much she loved his touch, how that, alone, was almost enough.

When she woke the next morning, the sun was already inside the blinds, tossing shadows of fish all over the bed. She raised up on one elbow and saw that the sofa was empty. So was the space on the floor where Keith's sleeping bag had been. Her pocketbook, slightly open, lay on the small table where she'd put it the night before. She felt a sickening thud in her chest.

She slipped out of bed and looked in her purse. No money, no credit card. She rushed to the closet; their passports and airplane tickets were still safely locked in her suitcase, along with the traveler's checks she'd insisted on bringing, though Miles had laughed at her for being old-fashioned.

When she came back, Miles was sitting on the edge of the bed reaching into the pocket of his pants where his wallet had been.

"You didn't hear anything?" she asked.

He shook his head.

"Thugs," she exploded. "Awful little thugs."

Miles nodded. "Well, they certainly fooled us, didn't they?" He sounded almost admiring.

He proceeded to dress as though nothing had happened. She kept an angry silence, which he didn't seem to notice, too intent on planning their last day on Crete. There was no point in reporting the theft, he explained. Ferries sailed hourly to Athens and other islands. Their thugs (a glance at her) were undoubtedly already on one. He would notify the credit card company, of course. But first, he wanted to see that minaret. She could find it again, couldn't she? He saluted her playfully. "Lead on, captain my captain."

"At least we ought to try to get those two arrested," she burst out—thrown in jail, deported, beheaded, she added silently. But Miles refused to listen. "Let's don't let them rain on our parade any more than they already have, for God's sake." So she gave up.

She led the way into the old town, Miles following her through the narrow streets that teemed with women carrying heavy bags, men on bicycles, the occasional *moto.* As for the minaret, she had only the vaguest notion where it was. Miraculously, in less than ten minutes, they were there.

"This is it?" Miles gazed up at the blocky old tower. He tried the door at the base; it was unlocked. "Hello-o-o. Anybody home?"

"Wait a minute," she said, her mind slowly beginning to function again. "Are we sure this thing's safe?"

"Worrywart." Miles flipped his hand at her. "Would they leave it unlocked if it weren't safe? After you, ma'am."

A terrible smell hit her when she started up the curving steps—urine, other unimaginable things. The tower was dark and airless, like a tomb. Her anger was replaced by alarm. If Miles had not been behind her, she would have turned back.

At the first gallery, she said, "I guess this is high enough."

He gazed calmly down at the jigsaw of dark roofs, then glanced upward. "I'll go first," he said, as if that made it all right.

Head down, concentrating on her breathing (thank goodness she'd taken yoga), she toiled up the stairs until at last she felt a waft of warm air and stumbled out onto the second gallery. She leaned against the tower wall, as far from the railing as possible. It was totally silent up here, no sound, not even the buzzing of Vespas, or "killer bees," as Miles had taken to calling them. She'd never dreamed she could miss them.

Miles stood by the railing, wisps of dark hair curling in the breeze. "Icarus once fell out of that sky, you know, Bun. Do you remember my telling you about Icarus?"

"Yes," she whispered. How could she forget? The boy with the wax wings who flew too close to the sun. Oh, that story broke her heart. The boy's own father had made the wings. How had *he* felt? She remembered a lot of what Miles told her, though she didn't talk about it.

"No one would try such a thing these days," he said. "Afraid they'd be fined for breaking some safety law."

She decided not to tell him again they shouldn't be up here, that it wasn't safe. She'd just be proving his point.

"Hey!" He was pointing out at the sea where a microscopic ship moved stealthily across the horizon. "There they go, God bless 'em. Off to see the world on our nickel."

So he *had* been thinking about Keith and Lisa. She closed her eyes. She did not want to think about them. Now that her anger had faded, a deep ache had begun. The trip had finally worn her down, the way it had Miles at the beginning, though now here he was, full of energy and hope.

She heard him chuckle. "I'm kidding about their being on that ferry. I'd bet the farm they're still in town, spaced out on their substance of choice. Well, we can't say we didn't know why they accepted our hospitality."

"What do you mean?" Her eyes flew open.

"Oh please. Don't tell me you didn't—Bun? Bunny!"

It must have shown in her face, her grief, her terrible chagrin. He'd *known?*

He was at her side in one stride. "Bunny, I'm sorry. I'm an ass—"

She gazed up at his large white face. "You *knew?*"

"Of course not. I just—We didn't lose much of value,

Bunny, a few hundred dollars, and to tell the truth, I enjoyed their company. I know it sounds insane. The girl was a mess, but the young man had some brains. Enough to rip us off royally—Sorry, sorry. We won't talk about that anymore. Lean against me. Good girl. I'm going to take you down now. Close your eyes. That's right. You'll be fine. I'll see for both of us."

She closed her eyes and let him guide her. Limply, she thought of the boy last night as he'd hinted of viciousness, though treachery was what he'd meant. And Miles had known, or at least suspected. Yet he'd never prevented her from bringing the children home, Keith and Lisa and all the others over the years, knowing there would be a price to pay. Oh, this wasn't the first time, though it was the worst—the first theft. Before, there was only ingratitude; rarely had any of her strays kept in touch with her or acknowledged the little cards she sent after they left the college.

She clutched Miles's arm as they moved slowly down the spiraling steps together, carefully putting her foot next to his on each next step. She inhaled warm air as they passed the lower gallery. They'd soon be on solid ground again. When they got back to their room, she would make coffee and they would sit on the balcony. The minaret, too, would be back in its place, a distant spire floating above the roofs, exotic, unreachable—as it should be. She should never have gone looking for it. What a fool she was.

Then she heard him whisper, his breath warming her ear, "We did it, Bun. You realize that? We're *here*."

What was he talking about? Where was *here*? This smelly old tower? But the tremor in his voice made her heart quicken. Miles often saw things she overlooked. She opened her eyes and there, at the bottom of the tower, was a circle of light, waiting for them.

"Miles," she said, "you know—"

"Shhh." His arm went around her shoulders. "Don't talk."

She had wanted to tell him what the boy said last night, that perhaps he'd been making an apology of sorts. But there would be time later to talk. They went on in silence, descending the steep and dangerous spiral, toward a sun-filled door.

About the Author

~

Born in Winston-Salem, North Carolina, Kate Blackwell is a former journalist. She now writes fiction and teaches writing at The Writer's Center in Bethesda, Maryland. Her stories have appeared in many venues, including *Prairie Schooner, New Letters,* and *The Greensboro Review,* as well as in several anthologies. She lives in Washington, D.C.

Photo by Mary Noble Ours